ELLEN ROGERS

WARREN ELLIS

NORMAL

Warren Ellis is the author of FSG's first digital original, *Dead Pig Collector*; the *New York Times* bestselling novel *Gun Machine*; and the underground classic *Crooked Little Vein*. He is also the award-winning creator of a number of iconic, bestselling original graphic novels, including *Red*, *Ministry of Space*, *Planetary*, and *Transmetropolitan*, and has been behind some of the most successful reimaginings of mainstream comic superheroes, including Iron Man. He has written extensively for *VICE*, *Wired*, and Reuters on technological and cultural matters and is working on a nonfiction book about the future of cities for FSG Originals. He lives on the southeast coast of England.

NORMAL

NORMAL

WARREN ELLIS

FARRAR, STRAUS AND GIROUX

NEW YORK

Farrar, Straus and Giroux
18 West 18th Street, New York 10011

Library of Congress Cataloging-in-Publication Data
Names: Ellis, Warren, author.
Title: Normal / Warren Ellis.
Description: First edition. | New York : Farrar, Straus and Giroux,
2016.
Identifiers: LCCN 2016025810 | ISBN 9780374534974 (paperback) |
ISBN 9780374712631 (ebook)
Subjects: BISAC: FICTION / Literary. | FICTION /
Technological. | GSAFD: Fantasy fiction.
Classification: LCC PR6105.L635 N67 2016 | DDC 823/.92—dc23
LC record available at https://lccn.loc.gov/2016025810

Designed by Abby Kagan

Our books may be purchased in bulk for promotional, educational,
or business use. Please contact your local bookseller or the Macmillan
Corporate and Premium Sales Department at 1-800-221-7945, extension
5442, or by e-mail at MacmillanSpecialMarkets@macmillan.com.

www.fsgbooks.com • www.fsgoriginals.com
www.twitter.com/fsgbooks • www.facebook.com/fsgbooks

1 3 5 7 9 10 8 6 4 2

PART ONE

Hand over the entire internet now and nobody gets hurt," she said, aiming the toothbrush at the nurse like an evil magic wand. The end of the toothbrush had been inexpertly whittled into what someone who'd only ever heard of a shank would think a shank looked like. Her hair was wire-brush gray, secured at the back by old brown rubber bands, and her left eye was twitching enough that she occasionally pointed the supposed weapon at a ghost image over the nurse's shoulder.

"Professor," the nurse said, head bobbing, working hard to make direct visual contact with at least one of her eyes.

The Professor was in her fifties, with the build and posture of an imperious bird, and spoke with a reedy voice most often used to control children and dogs. "I mean it," she said. "This is outrageous. Conditions here are medieval. I haven't seen a picture of a cat in six weeks and it is simply too much."

The nurse was a stubby stump of a man, with thick eyebrows, oaken muscles, and those middle-aged men's pores that gave him a permanent five-o'clock shadow. He bounced and glowered, looking to Adam Dearden like nothing so much as a cartoon gangster from children's television. Behind the countertop of the intake hall desk, another nurse, wearing what were evidently staff-uniform gray scrubs, weaved nervously. Adam felt panic squirm under the tarpaulin of medications in his system. He never expected the arrival at Normal to be the most stressful part of his day. "Professor," the stocky nurse growled again, "if you don't put that down right now, then we're going to have to take it from you. And that didn't work out so well for you last time, did it?"

"If you would just give me the internet I wouldn't have to keep making weapons. You are sorely trying my patience, young man. I agreed to none of this."

"Now, we both know that's not true, Professor. You agreed to it, your employer agreed to it, you signed the intake forms."

"What does it matter if I signed the intake forms? They wouldn't stand up in court. I'm clearly insane. I'm threatening your life with a toothbrush, for God's sake. A *ten-dollar* toothbrush."

The Professor looked at her own hand holding her own toothbrush. Adam Dearden's own nurse, a copper-headed strongman who'd said perhaps eight words to him on the trip, quietly took Adam's arm and pulled him away from the scene by a meter.

"I've quite ruined the damned thing," the Professor said, turning the toothbrush around in her fingers. "If you hadn't stolen my death ray I would never have had to resort to such extremity."

She sagged in her skin a little, and handed it over to the nurse. "I only wanted to see some pictures of cats. A GIF or two. That's all."

"We'll have you over to the Staging post in just a little while," said the nurse, who was a terrible liar and didn't realize that everyone he'd ever met knew it. "Let's go on down to the recovery station now, get you feeling better."

He gently took her wrist and began to lead her down the wood-paneled eastern corridor, away from the latex-paint greens of the intake hall.

"Can I have all of the drugs?" Adam heard her ask.

"This way," said Adam's nurse, bringing the number of times he'd heard that since the beginning of his journey up to a nice round ten. At PDX, the nurse had met him on the runway, Adam having been transported by private jet, and said, "Adam Dearden? This way."

Adam didn't know what the staff here at Normal Head had been told about him, for them to arrange his collection by a giant capable of circumcising redwoods with his teeth, but he had shuffled along meekly. It didn't seem productive to argue, and also he'd been shot full of so many sedatives and antipsychotics before he'd been stuffed onto the plane that he could not in any case have raised a persuasive enough argument to his legs to get them to do anything but shuffle. He felt like he might have to manually restart his own lungs at any moment, because relying on his body's autonomic functions was seeming more and more dangerous.

Perhaps unwisely, he had voiced this concern while being helped up into a ridiculous SUV with the footprint of a tank and a front fender apparently designed to atomize houses on impact, and was told to "shut up" in a tone that strongly suggested the nurse knew how to murder people really well. Adam shut up, and watched Portland scroll by, detached from the view to the point where he could have been sitting in a stationary vehicle on a set watching a back projection, or two people frantically cranking a roll of painted landscape to simulate motion. None of it seemed real. He laughed at Mount Hood, capped with silvered white in the middle of summer. Who paints a frosted mountaintop into a summer scene? What a ridiculous failure of reality.

He stopped laughing when he remembered it was a

failure of reality that put him in this car in the first place, and was quiet for a long time.

The oaks and firs stood up as they reached the interstate and pushed on through the South West Pacific Highway to the Salmon River Highway, past places with names like Falling Creek, Tualatin, Joe Dancer Park, and Erratic Rock. Places you could walk out into and die and never be found. He could imagine them seared by sun in summer and shrouded in snow in winter. Hammered by hail the size of coins in spring and autumn, pounding flesh and smashing bone, processed to be carried off chunk by speck in the guts of birds.

He had had a friend, a thin man with soft eyes and a tight jaw who ground his teeth whenever he was thinking, who'd walked out one day in a spare place like these. He'd left a note by the front left wheel of the pickup truck parked outside his cabin, pinned to the dirt by an old can of dog food. He was one of the generations who typed all day, and his handwriting had lost the fluency of daily practice. The note read, "You won't find me. I am returning to the cycle of nature while I still can. I don't want to see the end of the future. Tell my father I'm glad he has cancer. Goodbye." He had scrawled a drawing of an empty hourglass at the bottom of the note. Adam remembered flipping the note, and finding that it was scrawled on the back of a pharmacy receipt for a great many painkillers and four bottles of expensive mineral water, the stuff with extra vitamins in it. They never found him. Adam presumed that the empty plastic bottles of pills and water were still bobbing around in a creek somewhere, as a final fuck-you to the littering world his friend despised, while he circled overhead, riding legion in the bellies of birds.

It was after Erratic Rock—grassy floodplain that didn't look even a bit as interesting as the name—when Adam childishly asked if they were there yet. The nurse, who wasn't driving and was instead sitting and watching Adam like a cop guarding some heinous criminal during a prison transfer, said, "Not long," and that was the whole eight words done. He wasn't telling the truth, either, because it took another hour before they reached the eastern gate of the Normal Head Experimental Forest, out amid the coastal wilds of Oregon in the United States, where no one was watching.

The Normal Headlands were a conservation site, denoted both as a United States Forest Service Experimental Forest and as a UNESCO Biosphere Reserve. Inside the boundary of Normal Head Experimental Forest's thirteen thousand acres lay, over the bones of a ghost town called Normal Station, the Normal Head Research Station. Adam, like many of the people in his field, had heard of Normal Head—knew roughly where it was, had listened to all the stories about what happened there from friends of friends and the occasional fragile, wistful outpatient—but this was the first time he'd seen it. Seeing Normal Head up close was not a good thing for persons sharing his profession. Knowing what he knew, and having some awareness left regarding his own condition, he wondered if he'd see this gate again. He knew that there was a fair chance that he might never leave the forest. He knew that some people don't come back.

Adam was given to understand by the two guards at the eastern gate's checkpoint that he was causing them to miss the start of *Bonanza* on the television, and that he was therefore not their friend. Adam was a little sad about this, but only because he found he really liked the notion of sitting and watching an episode of *Bonanza*. There was something oddly soothing about the idea. His nurse growled at the guards. Adam suspected they weren't supposed to interact with him even that much. The two men grudgingly took Adam's photo, claimed that their various other items of security equipment weren't working, took a signature off Adam's nurse, and waved them through. It was difficult even to conceive of them as "guards," but Adam had taken direct and nervous notice of the large handguns in duty holsters on their hips.

The car drove on, down a long and winding track lined by unbroken curtains of vast trees that he supposed he would have time to learn the names of. He could pick out an oak, and had had Douglas firs pointed out to him during a previous trip to Portland, but otherwise trees in Adam Dearden's life went by the name "tree." There didn't seem to be much other than trees here, and he briefly toyed with the notion that he might be forced to live in one as part of his therapy. He didn't broach the subject with his nurse, partly because his nurse wouldn't be amused and partly because all communication since Windhoek seemed fraught with danger. He'd felt for days that he somehow wasn't making sense to anybody, and that everybody seemed to get angry or threatening whenever he spoke. So he looked out the window and invented names for the species of tree that he could discern.

That stopped being funny or distracting long before they eventually reached the Station compound. A Brutalist horseshoe of a building squatting on one side of a big square of bark-dressed dirt, opposite a stand of raised huts surrounded by odd little modular buildings that looked like they'd been parachuted in from five years in the future. The car stopped at the top of the horseshoe— its long arms turned away from the square and disappearing off into woodland—and Adam was caused to understand by one large nurse's hand that he was required to leave the car. Adam was oddly proud that it took the nurse a further five minutes to pry him from the car, and forgave himself the high-pitched screaming that accompanied the performance.

Of course, on being produced through the doors and into the intake hall, Adam was no longer the star of his own show. An older woman was demanding internet access at the point of a poorly sharpened toothbrush. The air crackled with nervous energy. Adam felt the stress headache start in his neck, and his eyes prickled with tears. Someone was asking him a question, he knew, but he couldn't quite make the words make sense. He recognized the tone of voice that defined the string of sounds as a question, which pleased him—not too far gone, eh?—but otherwise he felt like someone had stolen the internal dictionary that normal people used to match sounds to ideas. His chest went tight, and his chin bunched involuntarily. He shook his head, violently, and pain firecrackered up his neck and into the base of his skull. His brain reconnected long enough to hear the woman ask brokenly for drugs, and then, for no good reason he could find, he started crying. And couldn't stop.

When Adam came back to himself, he was outside, sitting down, with no memory of having gotten there. He was seated on a plastic chair, at a plastic table, with a plastic tumbler of something green in front of him. There was a woman seated opposite him, with cruel eyes and a kind smile. "You should drink that," she said.

The awful, sorrowful fugues tended to strip him of anything but "Where am I?" Which was a stupid question, but it was the only one he had, and it helped to level him.

"That's a big question," the woman said. "Technically, it's the Normal Head Research Station, but in 1910 it was Normal Station, founded by a realtor from Coggon, Iowa. They have a baseball team called the Rockets. Town motto, 'The One and Only.' Six hundred and fifty people live there, but they have an opera house. Imagine that. Well, the realtor bought this whole great big parcel of dirt, with the plan to turn it into a resort. He moved out here with his wife. There was a hotel here, housing, a small grocery store, even a printing press for a newspaper of record. In which it was reported, in 1913, that the realtor had gone, I quote, 'violently insane,' and had fled from what he described as, quote, 'the terrible lights of Normal' into the forest, never to be seen again. Between the wars, when the ocean began to eat into the shoreline, it was said that the sea came in at the point where the poor man left the land. By then, of course, Normal Station was empty. After World War Two, Normal Station became Normal Head again, the headlands were designated a forest reserve, this facility was opened in 1974, and we're sitting on the bones of a town founded by a madman whose last recorded words were about its terrible lights. That's where you are."

Adam reached for the glass. The woman talked in a flat and affectless style that unsettled him in ways hard to define. She was somewhere deep in the basement of the Uncanny Valley of faux-human speech. "I'm glad I asked," he said, and took a drink. Juiced shrubbery cut with lemon, cucumber, three millimeters of raw ginger, and some tinned fruit without properties beyond sugar. It tasted bad enough to bring him closer to the world.

He looked up at the woman again. "I know you. I recognize you."

"Ah!" she said, her smile widened yet never getting within shouting distance of her eyes.

She wore an expensive, oddly asymmetrical jacket, with zippered hidey-holes for gadgets and shades, and special gravity pockets in the sleeves that allowed the owner to slide her phone out of them into her hands like Robert De Niro's trick gun in *Taxi Driver*. She also wore steel-blue jogging pants, faded to white at the knees, and bulbous pink plastic clogs.

"We met at the Uplift conference in Brussels a couple of years ago. You're an urbanist. Lela Charron."

"That's right," she said, with a tiny hint of surprise. "And your name's Adam."

Suddenly feeling awkward, he stuck out his hand. "Adam Dearden. Pleased to meet you. Again."

She looked at his hand with eyes like a panther. "I don't really do touching of other people yet," she said.

"Sorry," Adam said, trying to yank his whole arm back into his body.

"It's all right," she said. "We all have our issues here."

"Here," he said, looking around. "Normal Head. I don't remember a lot about the trip at the moment. But I guess I made it. Will I see a doctor soon?"

"Oh, yes," Lela said. "They just like you to sit down with a long-term inmate and find your feet before they get into all that with you. They think it's best you see a nonauthoritarian face first."

"Inmate?" It made him smile a little.

"Patient, then. I've been here six months. I'm in Staging now."

"What's that?"

"When we're most of the way better, we get moved to Staging. You saw the micro-homes on the way in?"

"Those weird modular things?" Adam found he remembered that. That was good.

"Right. We live in some of those, use others as communal work areas. They have computers and internet. We're allowed to work there. Beginning the process of reconnecting to the world. Staging for a return to the outside."

"Have you been Staging long?"

"A couple of months," she said, turning and looking out over the grounds. They were on a wide patio area, filled with plastic tables and chairs. All injection-molded, cheap, and nothing but rounded edges. Beyond the patio, a scabby lawn, and then the treeline. Adam imagined running screaming toward it.

"That seems like a long time," he said.

"No," she said. "There have been people in Staging for years. Sane enough to be useful, never quite safe to leave. For some people, it's not a bad arrangement. Working from concealment, as it were. Me, I'm feeling ready to go back. Nearly ready. Do you know why you're here, Adam?"

He took another sip of the horrible green shit.

"Bad case of abyss gaze," he said. "You?"

Lela frowned. A small wet sound came from her mouth. She smacked her lips, and swallowed something. She wiped a scant escape of saliva from the corner of her mouth. "Poor culinary choices," she said.

There were people at most of the tables. Like the outdoor furniture, they slowly resolved in his perception, as if a contrast control was being turned up on the screen of his Cartesian theater. He also became aware of a wide gap that bisected the patio, an aisle between the tables.

Lela followed his eyes. "Professional demarcation," she said. "Foresight strategists on this side. Nonprofits, charitable institutions, universities, design companies, the civil stuff. On the other side? Strategic forecasters. Global security groups, corporate think tanks, spook stuff. You know the score."

Adam did. He was a futurist. They were all futurists. Everyone here gazed into the abyss for a living. Do it long enough, and the abyss would gaze back into you. If the abyss did that for long enough, the people who paid you for your eyes would send you to Normal Head. The place was paid for by foundations and multinationals alike, together. Most of their human probes needed it, one way or another, in the end. His first thought, in fact, that night in Windhoek, was that he was going to end up in Normal if he couldn't keep his shit together.

His neck pain came back.

He looked out toward the treeline again. There was a figure out there, moving among the trees, wrapped in a heavy black coat. Adam realized that he must have made an expression while looking, because Lela turned to see. "Oh," she said. "That guy. He's either in his room or wandering around the edges. He's on the other side. Strategic. No idea who employs him. I don't think I've ever even seen him speak to anybody. There are always one or two like him. You're probably one of the healthier specimens, as new intake goes."

"He's new here too?" Adam had the sudden aching feeling of no friends, an endless emptiness of childhood loneliness, and that perhaps someone else who was new to Normal Head might be a friend for him. It made him want to cry again, but just for himself and the ache and his childhood.

"Arrived a few days back, I think?" Lela said. "God knows what's wrong with him. Maybe he's checking out the trees for cameras. It happens."

"Checking out the trees happens, or cameras happen?" Adam felt the fuse light in the top of his spine. He blinked hard, a few times.

"Oh, there are cameras here. I mean, many of your fellow inmates are humans with significant dollar value attached to them. But not in the rooms. And the ones out here are pretty discreet. The video files they generate are on a forty-eight-hour deletion cycle. Their wireless is disabled, they don't have a hard line off-site, airgaps and high security and all that. They kind of have to. Working in and around surveillance culture for too long put a lot of these people in here, after all."

Nothing but true, Adam knew, especially for urbanists like Lela Charron. He'd seen them counting off every single networked object on city street corners, like botanists identifying every single obscure poisonous plant in sight. Staring into the abyss of the future while being acutely aware of being watched by every device, every piece of street furniture and every strand of modern infrastructure.

The trees sighed under a cold breeze, and the man in the heavy coat dissolved into the forest.

"Well," Lela said. "My work here is done. Finish your drink, it'll help you feel better. An orderly will come by in a little bit to take you to your doctor for your induction interview. Word of advice: don't try to be a big strong man. Or," and she cast him over with that raptor look again, "a little big man. Just be whoever you are right now. Don't be afraid to show them where you're broken. You'll get fixed quicker if they can see the breaks up front."

"That's it?"

"Yes, that's it. What did you want? A hug?"

A voice came from over Adam's shoulder, a deep and sooty sound choked up from the base of a tired throat. "She doesn't touch people because she ate one once."

Adam twisted in his seat. The speaker was a man from the north of England, by his accent, with a face like a mallet and skin like a map of Yorkshire scratched out in gin-broken veins. He wore a gray suit that might even have been gray when he first put it on, which Adam judged to have been a couple of years ago. The man's great head, inflicted with a bootneck haircut that Adam thought had been made illegal for reasons of cruelty by 1958, had the permanent inclination of a man too used to explaining to colliery housewives that their husbands and children had been eaten by a mine shaft. But a grin split it like a spade through clay.

"How do," the man said, sticking a sweaty hand out to be shaken. "My name's Clough and I'm fucking mental. So's she. Don't trust a word out of her cakehole."

Lela started hiccupping.

"Oh, here we bloody go," said Clough. "Did she start dribbling at the mention of food yet?"

She outright murdered Clough with her eyes.

"Don't listen to her, lad. She went straight-up batshit in Mongolia and they're never going to let her out of here because she's fucking mental and she's got a taste for human flesh."

Lela snatched the plastic tumbler out of Adam's hand, threw the juice out of it, and smacked it down on the edge of the table, all in one smooth and terrible motion. If the tumbler had been glass and the table had been wood, it would have instantly produced a fine makeshift weapon. But instead the tumbler made a dull thud on the side of the table, which tipped and rocked a little.

"Fu-UCK," Lela hiccuped, and threw the tumbler at Clough. She missed and hit Adam in the center of his forehead.

"That's quite enough of that, Ms. Charron," said a soft young man in a 4XL short-sleeved white shirt. His small hand rubbed agitatedly at the arrangement that covered his early-onset male pattern baldness. "You were specifically asked to leave the new patient in peace to drink his green juice and calm down."

Lela swallowed hard and looked away. "I was just practicing, she said. "Practicing for when I go to Staging."

"I'm sure you were. You walk away too, Mr. Clough. It's cartoon time in screen room two soon."

"Ooh," said Clough, bouncing on the balls of his feet. "Is *Danger Mouse* on? We haven't watched all of that DVD set yet. Will it be *Danger Mouse* again?"

"Only," the younger man said, "if you promise not to launch another critique on the realism of the treatment of the British Security Service in *Danger Mouse*. Off you go now."

Clough gave Adam's shoulder a quick squeeze. "Chin up, lad. The food's fair, they've got a shitload of DVDs, and no bastard can fucking phone you here. It's not so bad."

It was a bizarre thing to see Clough scamper off into the main building singing the theme tune to *Danger Mouse*.

"My name's Dickson," the young orderly said. "Pleased to meet you, Mr. Dearden. Your doctor's ready to see you now. Do you feel up to talking to a doctor for a little while? We prefer to do it on intake day, but if you'd rather sleep and do it tomorrow, we can do that too. What do you say?"

Adam thought the back of his head was going to explode. "I'm not even sure I can stand up," he said.

Dickson put his hand, too small for its owner but very clean and dry, under Adam's arm. "Let me help," he said quietly. "It's what I'm here for."

The room was very yellow. In a northern country, the color would have been called "sunshine yellow," because they weren't very sure what color sunshine really was. Adam supposed it could in fact have said "happy pus" on the tin. The walls had been painted within the year, the armchairs and sofas were relatively new, and the thick carpet had been both vacuumed and shampooed recently enough that he could still detect the scent of the soap.

Dr. Murgu was in substantially worse repair. A cut was delicately taped closed over her bushy right eyebrow, and a bruise on her left cheek was blooming like mandragora. She'd changed her white coat, but hadn't had time to change the blouse underneath. The loop of blood spatter had been smeared and reduced by wet paper towel, but not erased. She looked at her clipboard—Adam had yet to see a networked object here—and then up at him, straightening her back as she perched on the edge of the sofa and pulling up a smile from somewhere under whatever had happened to her earlier in the day.

"Adam," she said. "Can I call you Adam?"

He just nodded. This is how the cycle went. Emotional incontinence, and then hyperfocused on the environment but drained of words. No sensory input/output. Human-shaped camera. Two facets of terminal panic, he supposed.

"I imagine the whole process of getting here has been both exhausting and confusing. So I'm going to start by telling you what's been happening. You got very ill in Rotterdam, and your institute got in touch with us. We had you transported to Schiphol, which has a direct flight to Portland. We drove you straight here from PDX. Do you remember anything about Rotterdam?"

Adam shook his head. It was a bit of a lie. He knew he'd been at a conference about coveillance. Some happy solutionist idiot with banana-yellow glasses and hair like a startled badger talking about how watching the watchers makes for a balanced and benign social substrate. Yellow glasses like this yellow room. Yellow is supposed to make people feel good. He wanted to make people feel good about a surveillance arms race between the state and the populace. Adam remembered losing his temper. He didn't remember much about what he said, except that it seemed to upset a lot of people.

He remembered beginning to cry afterward. He wasn't sure where he was when it happened, but he figured it must have been a public space. He remembered hands, arms, being lifted.

"Okay," she said, making a note with a propelling pencil. "Do you know how it started? Your illness. The thing that upset you?"

"Windhoek," he said, almost choking on the word. "Namibia."

"Were you there during the riot?"

He nodded. Her pencil scratched across the paper. Without looking up from what seemed to be a very detailed note, she asked, "How are you sleeping?"

"I don't even know," he said. Her eyes snapped up. "I'm being honest," he said. "I was given a lot of medication yesterday. I think it was yesterday."

Dr. Murgu flicked the top sheet of paper on her clipboard up, skimmed the sheet below. "Yes. It looks like you had three separate episodes."

Adam took a deep breath, pushing the bases of his thumbs into his eyes. "I am trying to be honest because I know that the more information you have, the better you'll be able to help me, and I must need help because I've been shipped to Normal. That means I have to tell you that I've been seeing things that aren't there and sometimes I'm not completely sure what's real. Hell, I saw a man earlier by the trees here and I'm not sure he was there. Lela may have just been humoring me during a hallucination."

"What man?"

"Dark hair, big heavy coat? I think he saw me looking at him and he walked into the forest."

The doctor smiled. "It's all right, Adam. I think you saw Mr. Mansfield. He never takes that coat off."

"He was really there?"

"He certainly was. As much as he ever is. He's been

here a few days, but we haven't even been able to do his intake interview yet. He hates to be looked at, hides in that coat, won't communicate, and spends most of his time wandering the grounds. I'm not sure anyone's even seen him eat. So what I want you to understand from this, Adam, is that you are far from the most wounded person ever to enter Normal. And I note that you met Lela. Lela has issues with things like permission, and time. She'll be a good friend, but I need you to carry with you the knowledge that everyone is here for the same reason, Adam."

Adam shook his head. "Doctor, are you telling me not to trust anyone here because they're crazy?"

"Absolutely," she said. "You're all batshit."

Adam looked at her with total focus. She smiled. He gave a sudden burst of laughter.

"There you are," Dr. Murgu said.

It was like all the air rushed back into him. His chest filled and his heart started beating again. His skin stung.

She leaned forward, keeping the eye contact. "Adam, you've had a nervous breakdown. I know it's been a tough couple of days. But you're here now, and things start getting better for you right this minute. You're going to have some bad moments, because your mind is wounded. But they are going to get less and less frequent. This is a safe place. No prying eyes, no pressure, no eavesdropping, no agenda. You can start looking away from the abyss now."

Even he was tired of crying again. It didn't feel better. It was just exhausting and boring.

Dickson led him to his room. It had a window with a strong mesh over it, a single bed, and an armchair. There was a partition, with a toilet, sink, and shower packed into it. No desk. No expectation of work. The armchair suggested peaceful hours of quiet reading. There was a television and a soundbar mounted on the wall, and a heavy-looking remote control on the bedside cabinet.

Dickson saw him see it. "Music," Dickson said. "You can't get actual television. The remote has a slide-out keyboard, and the television shows the selection menu. Just music. No movies, no shows. No web access, of course. We got a ton of music, though. Lot of relaxing stuff."

"Any books?" Adam asked, eyeing the chair.

"Dr. Murgu will evaluate you for library access at your next interview. Over here."

Dickson directed Adam's attention to the door. On the back of it, a key hung by a yellow loop from a hook.

"That's your room key. You can lock yourself in. Please don't leave the key in the lock."

"Okay," Adam said. He was tired now. His eyesight was juddering.

Dickson produced a small plastic bottle from his chest pocket. It contained three capsules. "You need water?"

He did, and was made to stand in the doorway to the mini-bathroom while Dickson drew a plastic cup of water from the sink. The capsules were red, yellow, and green. Adam studied them on his upturned palm, where Dickson had laid them, and looked askance at Dickson.

"I know, man," Dickson said. "Stop, wait, go. Don't read anything into it. It's just the colors they come in."

Dickson observed Adam take the capsules, so closely that Adam felt he needed to swallow as ostentatiously as possible to satisfy the orderly's invigilation.

"Okay," Dickson said. "You need to eat?"

"I think I just want to sleep. Is that okay?"

"That's fine, Mr. Dearden. How are you with phones?"

"Um. I know how to use them . . . ?"

Dickson stepped to the bedside cabinet. "It's a real question. Some of our guests come in with a serious aversion to phones. They can be like a huge symbol of everything that's weighing on them? Someone told me once that it's hard to talk when you don't know how many people are listening. Like phones are half-trained demons always ready to betray you."

He opened the front of the bedside cabinet, where a cordless phone sat on a cradle. "It's a closed system, you can't dial out. And no one can dial in, obviously. Just hit '0' to get the front desk if you need anything. If you can't face that, press the green button on the TV remote. No audio recording."

"That's it?"

"Well, there's a whole menu, but you look dead on your feet and the front desk will take care of anything you need tonight. I can walk you through the other stuff tomorrow. Get some rest. I hear you had a long journey."

Adam's entire life felt like lead in his bones right now. He couldn't manage more than a nod. Dickson smiled, with genuine and gentle kindness, and let himself out of the room.

Adam sat down and surveyed the room in silence. He supposed it was as close to a hermit's cell as you got these days, without disappearing into the frozen wastes with a spoon for digging yourself a cave with. Except that you had to pick your frozen wastes carefully these days, as you could probably get 3G service in chunks of Antarctica and the Arctic was full of drunken Scandinavians in headbands and television hosts in SUVs.

He took it in for a moment. No internet. No phone service beyond the front desk. No television. No news. No information flow at all. Just a music collection and, somewhere, a library he evidently had to be medically fit to browse. It was quiet. It was actually quiet. He couldn't even hear other people. This little room was as close to sensory deprivation as he'd experienced since . . . when? Childhood?

He sat there for a little while, feeling like he was waiting for his ears to pop from the change in pressure. It came to him that he didn't even know where his cell phone was. He wasn't able to tend the eight different messaging apps on it. He couldn't clear the email from either of his accounts (one open to anyone, one that was nominally private but which suffered significant bleed-through from the other). No Twitter, no Instagram, none of the public-facing services he farmed hourly. No podcasts! He was subscribed to a hundred podcasts. He winced at the gigabyte load that would be waiting for him when he retrieved his phone and reached some signal. The news apps would spin and churn away, kicking out notifications until the phone's battery was sucked dry. His quant band was gone, he noticed: he wouldn't be tracking his steps, his blood oxygen, heart rate, local EF field activity, or the five other things it automagically quantified and uploaded and shared. Digitally, he would actually appear dead. A few of his services would send updates to social media daily. The weather report in his last recorded location would post to his Tumblr every day on an automatic basis. After a while, it'd look like an arrow pointed at the spot where he'd vanished or been murdered.

He didn't know where his laptop was. He didn't know when it'd last been backed up to his three off-site storage services. Christ. He was cut off, really cut off. It was an amputation. He realized he had no idea what to do with that. He was a cauterized stump of a human, dropped in a small room and left to rot.

A small room that bore the weathering of human presence as a slow tide lapping a beach of stones, rather than the marks of occupation. It was the sort of experience he had in low-budget hotels outside airports. He wondered if, in times past, there were caves in nowhere places that travelers used for only one night, on the way to somewhere of consequence. On their way home.

He sat there and thought about what home meant. "Home," in his life, was the word given to the house his parents had lived in. Adam didn't get to have one of those. Where they were was "home," and where he was was always somehow somewhere else.

Adam remembered the first time he'd been in a room like this. The first time he'd ever stayed in a hotel. Remembered lying there on the weary bed, atop a tired brown counterpane, thinking he'd made it. Finally staying in a real hotel. No more hostels and sofas and floors. A real hotel room, bought without pain with his own money. He remembered feeling like he was a big man now, on his way up. Things were just going to get better.

The capsules woke up in his gut and told the stump of Adam Dearden to go to bed, and so he did. They even took care of the shaking, though he would have sworn that his bones were vibrating inside the dead meat of him, desperately trying to generate enough electricity to capture a radio broadcast from somewhere.

It was the banging that woke him up screaming. It sounded like the percussion of explosives in the street. Something was going on outside. Adam leapt to the window. Pale daylight. Early morning, maybe. Nothing else. The banging was coming from the corridor. Adam had nothing that might constitute a weapon, except possibly the soundbar on the wall. His instinct was to yank it off the wall and use it as a club. He swallowed the instinct down. Adam pulled on his pants, as quickly as he could. His hands were shaking. He stepped to the door, quickly and silently, and took the key off the hook. He unlocked his door as quietly as he could, and wrapped the key loop around his wrist.

Adam cracked the door open. Two orderlies ran past. Whatever was happening, it wasn't about Adam.

Adam left his room and followed them. They had already stopped running. There were three more orderlies at the end of the hall, banging on a door. One of them turned to the new arrivals, and said, "You bring the persuader? Asshole left his key in the lock and he's not answering."

"You sure he's not out in the fucking woods again?"

"We already checked the corridor cameras. He went in at curfew and never came out."

The smaller of the two orderlies who ran past Adam produced something like a shorter version of the old spiral ratchet screwdriver his dad used to use when he was building things in the garage. Adam walked up to watch. They were all too busy to pay any attention to him.

The orderly put the device, which Adam presumed was the "persuader," to the lock, grasped the handle, and pumped it. Its mechanism clicked and spun and the lock barrel was kicked clean out of the door. He pulled a thin, pick-like tool out of the top of the persuader's handle and applied it inside the hole left by the lock. There was a loud snap. The orderly looked at his colleagues, and then gave the door a gentle push. It opened soundlessly.

He said, "Mr. Mansfield?" The door swung wide.

The orderly said, "Jesus *fuck*," and backed off. Adam stepped in to see.

The bed was host to a black and heaving mass of insect life. So was the floor around it. So were the walls, and the window. There was no sign of anything human in the room. The mound on the bed was just a horde of bugs.

Behind Adam, Clough coughed, squinted, and glumly observed, "I've fucked worse than that."

PART TWO

Adam Dearden hadn't realized how many people worked at Normal Head until Mr. Mansfield disappeared from his room. Half an army of orderlies, doctors, and security guards manifested from nowhere and filled the halls.

The patients had been woken or retrieved and placed in a large canteen space to be counted and held. Adam was sharp with shock, the fog blitzed away by the last half hour of panic and the unexplained. They weren't being told anything, and Adam had been specifically admonished by half a dozen extremely tense strangers to not say a word about what he'd seen until directly authorized to. Like an NDA, only scarier, because the people issuing it had access to medical equipment and he was trapped in a hospital in the middle of nowhere with them.

And yet. Mr. Mansfield had apparently either executed a daring midnight escape or received a thrilling rescue, leaving nothing but a pile of insects, presumably gathered and stacked while out in the woods, in his Houdini wake, as some kind of arcane insult. And nobody had any idea yet how he'd done it, because there were no cameras in the bedrooms at Normal Head. Only in the corridors, the public, and the outside spaces.

Adam sat down, on the northern edge of the room, as far away from the huddle as he could get. How *had* he done it?

Adam looked at his hands, and discovered they weren't shaking. The red, amber, and green capsules must've been some good stuff. Because—and he quietly, gingerly tested this on himself for the first time, letting the thought crest like a shark's fin in his mind—the whole event had a little bit of a Windhoek vibe for him. The night of the riot.

Those capsules, he decided, looking at his still hands, were the shit.

Adam turned his eyes up and cast them around the room. He supposed this was the entire strength of Normal Head, every single inmate. There was a different separation than earlier, though. Two large groups, dividing the room, yes. But there was a smaller group at the back, working hard to sit apart from everyone else. Adam twisted in his chair to get a better view of them. People were looking at them, but they weren't making eye contact with anyone but each other. And they all had wet shoes or slippers. They'd come from outside. Adam supposed they could be the "Staging" people—still inmates, but in preparation for release into the outside world.

But the others were split as before, right down the middle of professional demarcation. Being able to give them a proper once-over now, he began to recognize faces here and there, on both sides. He was scrupulous in avoiding any acknowledgment of recognition with any of the strategic foresight people. Not that many people in the room had the mental fortitude for direct eye contact anyway.

"All communication is dangerous," said Clough, plummeting into the empty chair beside Adam and knocking free his personal cloud of fossilized sweat. "Just fucking looking at someone constitutes communication. Especially if you want to shag them."

"Hello, Mr. Clough."

"Just Clough. It's a good bloody name, Clough. Honest name. Not like names these days. There are probably kids in this room called Wheat. Or Skylar. Or Sky*ler*.

Because it turns out they made a name up and never decided how to fucking spell it. I'm an economist, you know."

"What side?"

"Foresight strategy, pal. Nonprofit economic think tank in Eindhoven. Fucking *field* economist, I am."

"How does that work?"

"I go to big conferences and get important people so drunk that they can't shit straight, and then ask them evil questions and write down the answers."

"That," Adam offered, "doesn't sound so bad, really."

"It's bloody great," Clough agreed. "Except that when you get these bastards shitfaced they tell the truth. And it's fucking horrible. Over and over again. That last recession? That was practically fucking victory condition. We teeter on the brink of world financial ruin and a return to the days of trading fucking seashells for food, every fucking day. Worse. It wouldn't even be like *Mad Max*. Do you even comprehend how sad that is? Nobody runs Bartertown. That's the thing, lad. It's a runaway process. The absolute best thing anyone can do is grab desperately at the throttle. But they don't. Because it's a speeding death kaleidoscope made out of tits."

Adam looked around for Dickson.

"Tits," Clough emphasized. "It just dangles tits out everywhere. And tits will hypnotize a man. He'll just grab at them and suck. Unless," he reflected, "they like cocks. In which case just imagine a whirling thresher of cocks. Tasty ones. People just want a taste. And when they've had it, they want more, and bugger tending or directing the machine after that. They just crawl all over the thing, trying to drain it of its juices. Its terrible fucking juices, lad."

Adam spotted Dickson, who looked very harried and sweaty. Adam tried to look a little scared as he waved. Dickson saw it and changed his trajectory.

"Did you know," Clough continued, in a broken voice, "that more than half of the top nought point one percent—not the One Percent, the Nought Point One Percent—of the highest-paid people in America are financial professionals? Tits. I'm telling you. Draining the brake fluid out of a spinning machine that's going to shred the planet. I'm a fucking economist, me."

"Mr. Clough," said Dickson.

Clough wiped his eyes with trembling fingers. "I'm all right, son. I'm all right."

"If you need some help, just flag someone down, Mr. Clough. There's no shame in it. Everyone here is in the same boat, remember?" Dickson nodded at Adam and resumed his course.

"You've got it together pretty well," Clough remarked. "You were a crying zombie last time I saw you."

"I think it's the pills," Adam said.

"Yeah? Not the adrenaline, then?"

"No. The pills. I'm not liking this. Or being kettled in one place with all these people."

One of Clough's grimly untrimmed eyebrows rose. "Kettled. Spent some time in the field, eh? Done a riot or two?"

"Yeah. Don't really want to talk about it."

The street-protest checklist. Phone in a rugged case, in the front pocket of the jeans, screen turned inward. Slip the wristwatch off before you go outside. Enough adhesive bandages and painkillers (ibuprofen *and* acetaminophen) to share.

Fog. Fire. The stink of frightened people stampeding.

"What were you doing in the corridor?" Adam said. "When they were opening the guy's door."

"I don't sleep much," Clough said, breathing through whatever pain had been sharpening itself on his bones. "They're okay with me going for a walk so long as the sun is up. Which it is, just fucking barely."

"So why were they trying to get him up?"

"Everyone's on a different schedule. They're pretty good here, the staff, you know. If you get up with the sun and go to bed with it, they'll do their bit and come and get you at dawn and put you to bed at sundown. He might well have been one of them. God knows we never saw him around much. Aye aye," Clough said, nodding at the door. "Here we go, then. That's the Director."

A small, lean man around forty, who was evidently quite convinced that keeping his hair very short was hiding his male-pattern baldness. Stubbly and jittery, and yet bound inside a buttoned suit that was slightly too small, a look that bespoke his intention that everybody should know that he went to the gym a lot. He was flanked by medical staff, half of whom had clearly been rolled out of bed, all of whom were substantially freaked out. He showed a small limp as he moved to the front wall and faced the group, his staff fanning around him like courtiers in white coats and green scrubs.

"Your attention, please," said the Director, in a wobbly whistle of a voice. The room quieted. Glasses were adjusted, bodies leaned in. A few notebooks came out.

"Just after dawn, according to his personal schedule requests, staff attended the room of one of our guests, a Mr. Mansfield, for his wake-up call. As you know, we consider the privacy of your personal rooms sacrosanct, and so they didn't, as many of you are so fond of claiming, just barge in. A few of you may have been woken by their attempts to waken Mr. Mansfield. Eventually, according to protocol, they attempted to gain entry to the room. The door was locked and could not be operated. Again, according to protocol, the lock was defeated. My staff then discovered that Mr. Mansfield was missing."

He paused. Adam watched his jaw work. The Director was grinding his teeth.

"The grounds," he continued, "have been searched, and the security footage has been reviewed. Mr. Mansfield is gone from Normal Head, and there is no record of his transit."

The Director let that settle upon the room like fallout snow. The silence crackled.

"The room was locked. The windows were sealed, and the seals are still intact. As you know, we don't have cameras in your rooms. But outside your rooms the camera coverage is enough for us to be relatively certain that nobody intruded into our grounds and nobody left. This, however, leaves us with our central problem. Mr. Mansfield is missing. We presume Mr. Mansfield to be either abducted or deceased at this time. If our security was in fact somehow porous enough to let one person in, it may prove porous enough to let two people out."

"Why do you presume him abducted?" came a voice from the back, a man from the Staging group who'd arrived swaddled in seven layers of winter clothing. "What if he just broke out?"

"We are operating on a basis of information sequestration at this time. We have reasons for the hypothesis. That's all I'll say right now."

"Why?"

The Director sighed, and looked at the speaker as if

he was a child whose mother drank toilet cleaner during her pregnancy. "Because it remains entirely possible that someone in this room was involved with the crime."

There was a rumble across the room.

"Come on," said the Director. "You are all completely mad people who mess around with technology and weird social theory for fun until your brains shit themselves and you fall over. Any of you could have done this."

The medical staff stared at the Director in outright horror.

"What?" the Director snapped. "Am I telling stories out of school? Was it a secret that I preside over a large sweaty pile of people in a useless fake profession who somehow didn't have the mental fortitude to play pretend in return for paychecks all day? While I, Chief Asswiper to the Thought-Leader Elite, have to pay for three evil children, two shitty houses, and one supposed woman who stopped fucking me five years before she threw me out, literally, onto the street, where I was hit by some fat neckbeard on a Vespa so now in addition to all of the above I have to pay for five stupidly costly medications prescribed just to stop me from shrieking like a stuck pig all fucking day. And your issue is what? That I am revealing to people who piss their pants if they see a TV remote that they are in fact so damaged that they piss their pants if they see a TV remote? Eat shit and die. One or some or even maybe all of our precious inmates lifted another patient out of his room in the dead of night and probably fucking ate the poor bastard. Well, it doesn't matter. Normal Head is on lockdown and in the morning we are calling out for a specialist investigative team. Staging privileges have been pulled. Go to bed. Tomorrow we begin working out exactly who decided to ruin my life."

The Director left as soon as his last word bounced off the back windows, at a fast limp.

"He might be the most mental person here," Clough observed.

There was a lot of outrage and discontent in the room. Adam tuned it out. He replayed the pertinent parts of the Director's rant in his head.

Obviously, he knew what had been redacted from the statement. That awful roiling pile of insects that some comedian had left on the bed. But, even though they were spreading over the bedroom when Adam got his look at the scene, he'd never seen *under* that pile.

Adam's vision blurred, and his hearing began to wow like a distorted vinyl record. That seemed to be the end of his allotted thinking time. Everything started to get foggy around the edges. He jerked his head upright, trying to keep it above water and in full consciousness. Clough stood up and then leaned into Adam, seeing that something was wrong. But all Adam could see was someone looming out of the fog at him, and he started screaming, just like he did in Windhoek.

Adam Dearden found himself back in his room, in his chair.

Clough was sitting on the edge of Adam's bed. Lela was sitting on the floor opposite Adam.

"You fell down the abyss again," she said. "Shitty thing to have happen on your first night here, I guess."

"They let us sit with you," Clough said. "They've got their hands full. Lots of people are losing it."

"And," Lela added, "we're among the healthiest people here. We totally would have been moved to Staging soon. At least, *I* would."

"Except that they're going to pull Staging's privileges in the morning," Clough chuckled. "They'll lose their internet connection, and might even be made to move back into rooms in the main building. That tossed a big fat cat among the pigeons. They can cause trouble, and taking Staging away is one less incentive for people in here to stay on their meds and work through their issues. I would say the people in Staging are going to go nuts, but they already are."

"That's not true," Lela said. "Most of them just aren't ready to go back outside yet."

"You've met Colegrave. Tell me he's not insane. Tell me Bulat isn't insane."

"Hi," Adam said.

Lela glared at Clough, as if to say *That was all your fault*, and then put her attention on Adam. "How are you feeling now?"

"I should probably take some more pills?"

"No, lad," Clough rumbled, standing up. "Get some more sleep. This can all wait 'til breakfast. Which is probably in five fucking minutes, but still."

"It was nice of you to get me back here. Thanks."

"Can you answer a question?" Lela said.

"I can try." Her undiluted attention made him nervous. It was like having his movements studied by something fast and poisonous.

"Clough doesn't know you. I dimly recognize your name. But when we picked you up and started walking you out, someone from the other side called you by name."

Adam rubbed his eyes, faked a small yawn to buy a few extra seconds to search his memory. *The other side*. She meant strategic forecasters.

"I dunno," he said, pulling up the most well-worn weapon in his deflective arsenal by pure habit. "I've done a lot of conferences. I mean, we all do. I've done some cross-pollination things that had corporate attendees. I probably got recognized because of one of them."

"You gave materials to spooks? You can't do that. You can't talk about what you do and think. You can't publicly publish real stuff. That just gives them new tools to bring to bear on the streets. Every word out of your mouth to those fuckers can help cause pain to thousands of people. They give it all to the intelligence state. They do."

"Hell, no, I don't do that," he said. "You just go and listen. Those things are usually about operational security. The Chief Technical Officer of the CIA shows up with a slideshow, people theorize about Firechat and the blockchain, and you sit and listen and make notes, you know? And if you talk to people in the bar afterward, you just tell them you're writing a book or something. It's not a big deal."

"I don't do those conferences," Lela said.

"Well, you're a specialist," Adam said. "You shouldn't be in a place where you talk to authorities about how cities work. I'm more of a roving field researcher. I don't have a specific expertise I can be trapped into giving up."

That seemed to Adam to almost satisfy her. Almost.

"I need some sleep," Adam said.

"Yeah," Lela said. "Right. I've got things to do too."

Adam pushed himself up and over to his bed. "Yeah. We all do."

Lela was standing by Clough at the door when she

registered what Adam had said. "What do we all have to do?"

Adam laid himself out as if being fitted for his coffin. "We have to find out what happened in that room. Or else we'll all be trapped here forever and everyone will think that all of us died."

It was late morning when Adam made his way to the patio. He'd only stopped and cried once on the walk there, and didn't even feel insulted as he saw the shoes and slippers of people just walking around him as he kneeled with his head on the thin carpet there. He watched an insect, some kind of tubby louse or beetle, crawl ahead of him on the plastic skirting board, its sectioned back fairly rippling with the thrill of beating one of the giant things that haunted his world at a footrace. Even as Adam shook and curled there, he found himself wondering what the journey was like for that fat little object. Humans must be so vast that they were difficult to focus the beady insect eye upon. Towering blurs of things, terrifying and unpredictable natural disasters on the move. Finding yourself inside one of their buildings, like being trapped on a prison planet, the grubby polystyrene sky almost within scaling distance if you were prepared to give up a significant part of your life to such an insane task. If the creature made it outside again, it might be like emerging into orbital space, the next building as far away as the moon. It would take a human nine years to walk from the Earth to the moon. Wind as cosmic rays. Rain as meteor swarms.

He found an empty table, far toward the edge of the patio on the foresight side. Normal staff were very present. Adam watched them move among the tables, touching people on the shoulder, dipping their heads to speak quietly, offering smiles, writing in notebooks with gel pens when complaints were raised, passing out corn-plastic bottles of juices and smoothies and water. The intent was to provide reassurance on several levels, blatantly so. The staff didn't even care that it was unsubtle. The staff wanted the patients to know that they were available and that they could see all the patients at all times.

Adam was shortly brought two bottles himself, one of some beige solution and one of water, both dewed from a refrigerator. He wasn't remotely hungry. He opened the bottle of beige stuff anyway, on the assumption that the medication needed something to work with. The experimental sip didn't go well. It was gritty, and had, at the very least, been processed near some almonds, dates, and generic laboratory vanilla flavor, even if active doses of same had never made it into the finished food-substitute product. He wondered if it was Ensure or Soylent. The label on the bottle claimed it to be fresh-pressed, but there was no indication of the year that that was supposed to have been committed in. He began picking at the corner of the label. He thought about eating part of the label, in case it contained more nutrition than the beige muck. He didn't, because he thought it might make him look crazy.

Lela appeared in the chair on the other side of the table. "What do you mean, *we* have to find out?"

"What?"

"The last thing you said before you slipped into a coma. We have to find out. Or we're all going to be trapped here. What did you mean?"

She hadn't changed her clothes.

"I don't know," Adam said. "Paranoia. Cynicism. They're going to have to put together some kind of investigative team, which will mean some level of co-operation between all the people who fund this place, and I don't even know how you begin to investigate something like that anyway. On top of that, whoever did the thing may already have what they wanted."

"You mean removing that Mansfield guy?"

"I mean Staging privileges have been pulled. And according to you, those Staging huts are the only places where people other than the staff have internet access."

She sat back. "Wow," she said. "You *are* paranoid."

"No. Well, maybe. But I work differently than you.

I've seen your presentations." He took another small sip of the beige stuff. His stomach spasmed.

"What's that supposed to mean?"

"Nothing. Forget I said anything."

"No." She had those raptor eyes again, and she tapped claws on the faded plastic tabletop. "Say what you mean."

Adam twisted the cap onto the beige muck and decided to open his water. "You have a bad case of data-ism. You assume that data constitute a miniature of reality. Data as the only way to measure any given state or event."

"Oh my God," Lela said. "You really are crazy. Thank Christ they brought you here."

"No more crazy than what you did in Brussels in 2012. All that work you did on waste transportation. You captured an entire city's sanitation process from goods purchase to landfill. You gathered all the data, and then what did you do with it?"

"I gave it to the city, of course."

"And what happened after?"

"No idea. My job was to gather the data. It's not like I was hanging out with spooks."

"Except that it wasn't really a job. It was a university grant. But you turned over all the data and your conclusions to the city authorities anyway. Because all you cared about was making your miniature of reality. Something someone could hold in their hand. You were blind to the before and the after. Big old case of dataism. Fuck me, this water is disgusting."

"It's high alkaline. It reduces inflammation."

"I think I'd rather be inflamed."

"Clearly. What is it that you actually do, Adam Dearden?"

"Field research. Other things."

"What other things?"

"What's missing from your miniature of reality in this instance, Lela?"

"Don't change the subject."

"Did Clough tell you what we saw in Mansfield's room?"

The idea of an absent datum made Lela's brow knit. "No."

Adam leaned in, lowered his voice. "Some funny bastard thought it would be a good joke to empty a bag of insects over Mansfield's bed."

"I don't even know what that means."

"What I said. Don't ask me how. Someone, or ones, spent God knows how long stuffing ants and spiders and cockroaches and other fucking creepy-crawlies into a bag just so they could upend it over Mansfield's bed before they left. We saw the lock to Mansfield's door get punched out, and we saw them open a room, and we saw insects all over the bed and walking all over the room. I saw it. Clough saw it. Okay?"

Lela let the idea dance around her like a boxer, weaving in her seat. She took Adam's water from his fingers and stole a gulp.

"Why would anyone do that?"

"I'm paranoid, remember?" Adam smiled.

"Indulge me, crazy person. Since I'm an inflexible Puritan who only listens to the data. Tell me the news from Crazytown."

Adam took his water back. The bottle's rim had that odd warmth of another person's mouth that made him think of telephone hygiene supplies. He considered how to frame his response without exposing too much of himself. He reminded himself that everyone here was a little broken, and that made them all dangerous on some level. Also, that his own relative calm was a chemical production that could close its curtains at any point.

"Psyops," he said.

"Bullshit," she said.

"Okay," he said, leaning back with his water bottle, out of her reach.

In some form of abstract retaliation, she took the bottle of beige shit. "I'm having your smoothie," Lela said.

"You're welcome to it."

They stared at each other. It became a staring match. Sociopolitical virtual arm-wrestling.

"Psyops." Lela smirked. "Really."

"Do you know anything about it?" Adam said.

"Do you? Or do you just listen to the tinfoil-hat brigade spout about it on internet radio? You sound like one of them," she said, nodding at the other half of the patio crowd. "Which brings me back to why one of them knew you by name. Crossing the aisle is seriously not appreciated here, you know."

"There you go," Adam said. "Binary thinking. It's either inside your field of measurement or it's not."

"You are really starting to piss me off," Lela observed. She took a drink of the smoothie, which, it turned out, she actually liked. "I'm so glad they have Buoylent here."

"Buoylent?"

"You know what Soylent is, right? The powder mix that gives you all your nutritional requirements? Half of the Bay Area's been drinking it for years. They make their own custom versions of it here. Buoylent is like a medical version for mood management. Tastes better than Soylent, too. Much less like drinking a hobo's sperm."

Adam drank off half the remaining volume of water in the bottle in one gulp, gasped, and said, "They hand out lithium smoothies at Normal?"

"Please," Lela said with a curl of her lip. "This is the

twenty-first century. They're not going to poison us with lead any more than they're going to stick leeches to us. Although, it has to be said, leeches are used these days as artificial veins during surgical reattachment procedures. It's all about the continuing capture and processing of data, you see."

Adam gave her a slow clap as she smiled. "Oh, well played, madam."

"I'm going to Staging soon," Lela said, smoothing the planes of her jacket down. "I'm an urbanist. I understand processes."

"You're not in a city," Adam said. "You don't know where you are."

"Oh, go on, then, new crazy person. Indulge me. Where am I?"

"You're in an asylum that's been turned into a combat theater."

"*Really.* What kind of combat?"

"Psychological operations."

"Bullshit. Someone disappeared, is all. Everyone's freaked out, but—"

"No, this is how modern psyops works. Like this. Cutting a man's head off on camera and uploading it to YouTube. That's not just a killing. The killing is, in some ways, the smallest part of it. It's the theater of cruelty. It's an emotional contagion. The victim's family and friends know about it. They can't help but know. They know that people are watching it online. They know that even when the video gets pulled, stills from the whole thing will circulate. There will be TV and newspaper stories. They know, walking down the street, that anyone they pass could have watched that person die. The terror of interpersonal engagement and communication. All communication becomes dangerous. The impact spreads, becomes sociocultural. Friction in the area they live in. Police and social services get involved. And the windows rattle in the halls of power. Retaliation is considered, and perhaps even enacted, but they're striking against asymmetrically posed forces that are highly mobile and indistinguishable from the air. Air travel is the vector of infection. It gets harder to use planes. Free movement becomes difficult if not impossible for certain people and regions. Innocent people get killed. Innocent people lose freedoms. The contagion spreads and spreads and nobody can disinfect it. And just when you think the fever is breaking and the infection is dying down— there's another beheading. Another weaponized psychological outbreak. On and on. And the material cost to the attacker is a knife, a phone, and a minute's worth of internet connection. Or an abduction and a bag of wildlife. Abduction, the disappearing of people, works in the same way. You see where I'm going with this? A missing guy, a locked-room mystery out of Agatha fucking Christie, and a pile of insects. And you didn't know about the pile of insects. That information was withheld. But you know it's working on their heads, the Director and his staff and whoever they're all dealing with right now. And the first impact result is that we're now an electronic island. Who benefits from that? Who's happier knowing that the staff are paralyzed by fear, uncertainty, and doubt and that the presumably far-saner-than-us people who work in Staging now can't speak to the outside world in any way? You want to go at this from the perspective of dataism? The fact that Mansfield's body was apparently magically swapped with a stack of wood lice is a datum that was so fucking weird that the staff had to withhold it from the patients, and so until five minutes ago you had an incomplete model of the event and could not begin to process it correctly. Your little fucking miniature train set of the world had some missing tracks and plastic trees. Which it always does, because the world is not a train set, and dataism is bullshit, and you are as much of a threat to the world as anyone over there on the strategic foresight side because you don't actually know what you're fucking doing. You might think they're evil, but they think you're dangerous."

Lela grabbed his hand. He stopped talking. He discovered that he was shaking, and that he couldn't stop it.

Adam forced a trembling laugh. "I thought you didn't do touching of other people yet."

Lela looked at their hands. Her mouth tightened. She was making herself squeeze his hand, forcing herself over some kind of personal wall. "You looked like you were about to fly apart at the seams. I recognized the way you were talking because I still do it myself sometimes."

"Why are you here?" Adam asked, quietly.

She faked a rueful smile, and pulled her hands away. "Bad case of abyss gaze."

It would have been cruel of Adam to push. But he found that he wanted to be cruel. Just for a minute. Just for a tiny bit. Just enough to see a wound open and see a little blood. He wanted to hurt Lela, to graze her. To see if he could, and to toss a coin's worth of payback into the conversation for the times her tone and attitude had made him feel bad. Adam knew it was childish, but he rationalized it in this way: carelessly harming other people was a decent stand-in for baseline human interaction.

"I'm guessing that that's what we all say," Adam said. "What really did it? What broke you and put you here, Lela?"

"I'm not broken," Lela said.

"But you're here. You were staring into something that got you locked up here. What was it? Did the data fail you?"

"No." Lela's hands whitened around the bottle of Buoylent. "The data never fails me."

"And that was the problem," Adam said, working the tip of a knife into that tiny, nearly-but-not-quite-healed nick on her heart.

"That's the problem. You spend all day thinking of cities as machines for living in. And as the data piles up, and you realize the scale of the problems that cities are intended to solve, you start thinking of the city as a suit of armor to survive in. I mean, in theory and practice, that's exactly what it is. That's why cities used to have earthworks and walls around them. A city's supposed to have everything in it that its citizenry needs to live. If I'm sick, and I live in a city, it's almost certain that the care I need is closer to me than if I lived in a house in the country, because all the hospitals are in big towns and cities. People in what we think of as a basic Western city simply live longer. Basic, not, you know, collapsing or feral. Basic. Which means they fill up with old people. Huddled up against the health services they need and can afford, and all the other civic machinery that keeps their spaces livable."

Her voice was speeding up, and taking that flat, affectless tone he heard yesterday. Adam put his hand on the table, where hers had been, open. "I'm sorry. You don't need to go on."

"I do, though. I do need to go on. Because you need to hear it. Everybody does. I have to track shit, to do my job. Literally. I literally had to track the passage of shit through pipes in five major cities for six months, at one point. The way we move shit around in cities is fucking vital. It affects the condition of the urban environment, the volume of humans that can be supported therein, the quality of the water and the state of the ecology outside the city. At *least*. And then, yes, I had to hand over my data to the city authorities, because that's what I was hired to do. I don't get to make the decisions. All I can do is overwhelm them with data and reports until they have no choice but to do the right thing. But they don't, because nobody can hold the right thing in their heads. It's too big. It's too big and it's too deep."

"Lela, don't," Adam muttered, looking at the table.

"You know what I'm talking about. They"—she cast her hand across the gathered mass of people on the patio—"all know what I'm talking about. I got sent to New York. Fucking New York. They pump more than thirteen million gallons of water out of New York every day just to keep the fucking subway running. So that people can perform ten thousand felonies a year on it. And that's the small number. New York needs to pump another two hundred million gallons of water out of four thousand five hundred acres of city every single day to stop the city from drowning in its own piss and bathwater and the sea creeping up to grab at the ankles of the two million people south of Seventy-First Street. That is one system. Only one. And just in Manhattan. The five boroughs have to process more than a *billion* gallons a day. Remember Hurricane Sandy? Sandy took out half the pumps and almost all the treatment plants in a fucking second. And it was just barely a Category One hurricane when it hit. A thirteen-foot surge over the wall by Battery Park. That released ten billion gallons of raw sewage into the city and the surrounding waters. Shit. Big storm comes and we can't protect ourselves from our own shit. That's the future, Adam fucking whateveryournameis. City-states rammed with aging people huddling up against hospitals and looking up in terror for the big storm that will come and go and leave them floating facedown in thirteen feet of shit. And I can't do anything about it."

Adam was hunting Dickson with his eyes, which, if nothing else, kept him from accidentally making eye contact with Lela.

"None of us can. We just look at this stuff, we look wider and deeper, and then just deeper and fucking deeper, and all we can see is everything getting smaller and darker until it's this infinite black dot of compressed shit and horror. And we get paid for that. That's the amazing thing. We get paid to stare down the black silo of the future and gaze at the pebble at the bottom that's nothing but the crushed remains of the species. That's where we all end up. That's all we do. And there's a dollar value on that. We get given money for it. It's like we're the sin-eaters for the entire fucking culture, looking at the end of human civilization because it's supposed that somebody should. I'm fine, by the way. Stop looking for a nurse. I'm going to Staging soon. I'm going back to work. Society needs people to stare at a ball of shit at the end of the world all day. It's a living."

Dickson hove into view, a great galleon of a man sailing with peculiar grace through the archipelago of plastic islands between them. He arrived alongside their table with a puff of air. His eyes were rheumy and jittering.

"Mr. Dearden? I have to take you to your session with the doctor now. Are you ready?"

"I suppose," Adam said. "I guess I didn't know I was going to have one today?"

"Everybody's getting five minutes with a doctor at some point today. Come on up, sir. I'll walk you over."

Adam, standing up, went to say something to Lela, but she was looking away, robotically picking at the label on the bottle. Adam looked to Dickson helplessly, not knowing how to frame the question he thought he wanted to ask. Something about keeping an eye on her, giving her some help . . . something. He didn't know. He wanted to do something. Dickson nodded his head toward the doors, and Adam went with him instead.

"Must be a busy day for you," Adam offered.

"Yeah. None of us really got much sleep."

"You do look a bit tired."

"I am. Well, I was. Thank God they let us into the Adderall stocks. I could jog from here to Canada right now."

Dr. Murgu looked no better than Dickson, but she found a big smile for Adam. The clipboard in her lap had a few sheets of paper and a small pad clamped to it today. "Sit down, Adam. This is only going to take a minute, I swear. We're just checking in with everybody after the events during the night. Making sure it didn't do any damage, set anything off, that sort of thing. And I'm told you were actually there when Mr. Mansfield's door was forced open?"

A tiny spider was loitering with intent in the corner of the window. A spider with a Napoleon complex, not deigning to spin a web but hanging around on the insect street waiting to prove that he could beat the shit out of a fly with his bare palps.

"Yes."

"That must have been pretty awful."

"It was weird. I know the Director is sequestering information, and I don't know what else you've been told, so I don't know if I should really be talking about it."

Dr. Murgu studied her clipboard, with another smile, one that Adam couldn't clearly decipher. "That," she said, "was very operational-sounding. I think I've heard detectives on television shows say things like that. Makes it all a bit more dramatic and spooky, I suppose."

"I suppose. Maybe I heard it off the television."

"Maybe you did. So it didn't bother you unduly? Aside from, well, the strangeness of the thing itself? You don't necessarily feel better or worse today?"

It took her saying it for Adam to discover that he might actually have felt better today. "No, neither one nor the other," he said. "Aside from the strangeness of it all."

She made a note on her clipboard paper. Her smile went away. "I see. I'd like to ask you some more questions, but I have an awful lot of people to talk to today. We're going to adjust your meds a tiny bit, as your responses aren't quite where I'd like them yet. So, just relax today, and tomorrow we'll talk about the last week or two of your life in more detail. There are some gaps I'd like to fill. Okay?"

It wasn't okay. "Okay," he said. She scribbled something on the pad, tore the top leaf off, and handed it to him.

"Off you go, then. Take this. If you just step outside, Dickson will collect you, and if you give him that, he'll trot you off to the dispensary. Get some air, keep drinking the juices, and try a meal tonight. See you tomorrow."

Adam took it and stepped outside as directed. He felt like something had gone very, very badly wrong in the last couple of minutes.

Dickson trotted up, saw the script sheet, and took him to the dispensary window, where he watched Adam be served and take a plastic cup of capsules and tablets and a paper cone of water to wash them down with.

Another patient meandered over to them while Adam took his meds, with a sly gait. He was a well-lunched man in his thirties, plump and shiny like a British pork sausage, in port-colored corduroy trousers and the most appalling knitted sweater and pointed Nordic-style knitted hat Adam had seen since his last trip to Helsinki.

"Hello," he lied. Or, at least, that's how it sounded to Adam. "My name is Benedict Asher. You're Adam Dearden, yes?"

"Yes," Adam said, looking to Dickson, who was at this point chatting with the dispensary assistant about how they should be given Adderall every day because it was great apart from the tremors and the twitches and the teeth-grinding and the burning piss.

"Colegrave would like to speak to you. Over in Staging."

Adam discovered he was actually curious about Staging.

"Dickson," Adam said, "this guy wants to show me something over at Staging. Is that okay?"

"Hello, Ben," Dickson said, noticing the man in the stupid hat. "That's fine, but you'll need to bring Adam back, too. He doesn't know the layout of the place yet. I'm relying on you to do that, okay? We're a bit over-stretched today, and it'll be difficult to send someone over there to collect Adam. Do we have a deal?"

"Sure," Asher lied.

"All right, then," Dickson said, clapping Adam on the shoulder, "have fun and be careful." And, with that, he jogged off to the next job, leaving Adam with Asher. Asher had a twisty smile that Adam believed he could quite quickly learn to hate.

They walked through the main building together in silence, leaving by an exit Adam hadn't seen before. He was tracing the route in his head. He was pretty good with direction and space, generally. It helped when he was working on the street, particularly when things got bad. He was coping pretty well in Windhoek when . . .

Adam shook it out of his head and concentrated on walking and tracking.

The exit produced them into the open air, a few hundred feet from the edge of the woodland that seemed to wrap around Normal. On the treeline were clusters and stands of the micro-homes he'd seen on the way in, little bonsai houses with sloped roofs and plastic sidings, sitting on thick raised wooden decks.

As they angled toward one farther away and just inside the woods, Adam got glimpses through the buildings' tall windows. Tiny offices, enough for two or three people, cleverly compact kitchens, suspended stairs leading to upper sleeping areas. He spotted rainwater collection systems and tiny gray-water treatment plants. They were very self-contained.

There was still dew on the grass, which had been mowed a month or two back. He saw a few random dotted skeins of stepping stones, spotted mossy concrete discs set into the dirt, but the trampled lines of grass seemed to be the more popular footpaths.

They reached their target micro-home. It seemed like it might have been there longer than the others. Its sides were turning green, with thistles and blackberry vines tangling in evil possessiveness around the decking.

Asher stepped up and tapped on the glass door. Over his shoulder, Adam could discern the black shape of a figure draped in an office chair whose back was so tall that it might as well be a throne.

"Come," a voice intoned from within.

Asher popped the door and ushered Adam inside.

A man with the thinnest face Adam had ever seen said, "I am Colegrave."

Fingers as slim and curved as Turkish knives gestured at an empty smaller and lower chair across from the leather throne, which Adam took. The man wore an old black suit, quite well looked after, a crisp white shirt, and a flat black bow tie with the upper points tucked under the collars. And no shoes. After sitting, Adam put his heels to the floor and pushed his chair another six or seven inches away from Colegrave, until he bumped up against a wall. The man had a bitter fragrance that seemed to drape around him like a thick blanket, and Adam wanted extra distance from the contamination zone.

Colegrave pursed his lips. Perhaps he was offended. "Beginnings," he said. "Beginnings are very important. First impressions, foundations, and basic tenets. I am the longest-serving patient in Staging. I have been here for fifteen years. Do not display human facial expressions intended to denote sympathy. Fifteen years is nothing to me. I have lived for over a millennium, and, in all honesty, the food has never been better. I am the senior figure over here in Staging. This is a different world. This is

important. You have crossed into an alternative contin-
uum where the artificial separation between foresight
strategy and strategic forecast does not exist. We are neither one nor the other. Here, we are simply Staging. Are
you following me so far, Adam Dearden?"

Adam briefly wrestled with the pros and cons of asking for clarity on the thousand-year-old-man bit. Mea-
suring his own energy for it, he decided to let it ride.
Some things weren't worth wasting the braincycles on.

"I'm with you so far, Mr. Colegrave."

"Just Colegrave, please," he said, raising his talons.
"Basic honorifics will cease to be in the future that awaits
us, and I have discarded them in preparation for that
awful and glorious time to come."

"I see."

"Indeed. The crisis in time will be resolved. The project of democracy shall be undone, even unto the Magna
Carta. It's no accident that the Petition of Right and the
final usurpation of power by the English Parliament
were contiguous with the assumption of 'gentleman' as a
thing people could be and the word 'master' being taken
away from men of expertise and given to anybody.
'Master' became 'mister' and now we are all tainted by
the negation of correct civilization."

"Fifteen years in Staging, you say?"

Colegrave folded his hands over his dead knot of
a knee. "They will never release me. The work I do in

Staging is very valuable. And they know that if I were to escape into the outside world I would end it. It doesn't matter. It will end anyway. The pressure of time is inexorable. You've been here a day, correct?"

"Yes."

"So you are both insane and unlucky. Or insane and a hapless instigator."

Adam bristled without quite knowing why. "Instigator? Really?"

"You were the only new patient to arrive yesterday. Mansfield was taken last night. I'd be a damned fool to not consider the possibility that you had some involvement. He arrived two days before you, and, from what we can glean, had a meteoric career path in defense intelligence forecasting over the last two years. It certainly wasn't a rescue, since it was his own employers who sent him here, and would constitute a rather baroque suicide that spoke to an imagination he likely didn't possess."

Adam flexed his fingers. "Are you leading the investigation?"

Colegrave had a sudden harsh laugh like a fighting-dog's bark. Adam jumped from it.

"They would never even think to have me lead the investigation. The Director's an idiot. He was an idiot even before he was damaged. Any sane civilization would have terminated him humanely and processed his body for mineral reclamation a couple of years ago. Humanely, mind. I'm not a monster. They say I'm a monster, but I'm not. I'd use one of those bolt capture guns they use on cows. Very efficient. Instant death. The bolt immediately destroys the brain, you see, which is precisely the instruction given to police snipers in terror situations. Destroy the brain. It's quite the fascinating thing to think about, here in a compound in a forest where people with destroyed brains live. I imagine most of us will be put to death, when the world returns to its correct course."

Colegrave's voice had drifted off, become wistful, and he was stroking his own left temple with one fingertip, making it tender for the euthanizing metal bolt of the future.

Adam rocked on the back legs of the chair. It gave him a small nostalgic pleasure to do it. Memories of daydreamily pretending to be a stunt rider popping a wheelie while sitting in class during endless dull afternoons that seemed to be a bureaucratic conspiracy to steal the young years from him. "Colegrave," he said, "I had nothing to do with it. I just saw the aftermath. So did Clough. I don't see Clough in here."

"Clough is an economist, and therefore permanently mentally compromised long before he set foot in Normal Head. Also, obviously, the man is both an imbecile and demented, as well as a jackal at the feet of . . . anyway." Colegrave had come back somewhat from his execution fantasies and realized that he was losing Adam. "The

Director has summoned an investigative team, but that will take time to assemble and transport. Time that we cannot allow to drip away. We, ourselves, must investigate this event."

"I agree," Adam said.

"Of course you do," Colegrave smiled. "You are a man of both sides of the aisle, as it were. I looked you up when you arrived yesterday. When I still had internet. You're missing from a few of the usual lists and databases. I had to make some special queries. The Stoop Model is only the tip of your particular iceberg. There are a lot of people in Normal who were put here by paranoia and fear over the modern surveillance state, and I'm sure you wouldn't want questions about how deep your connection with it runs to be asked in the open air. Whatever happened to you in Windhoek must have been quite singular, given your work history."

Adam was very still.

"That said," Colegrave continued, "sometimes it is simply a case of one thin straw breaking an overstressed camel's back, isn't it? My point is simply this. There are three strains of human in Normal Head. Strategic forecast, foresight strategy, and Staging. It is therefore, apparently, a happy accident that we have one person able to speak to all three phyla of Normal Head patient. You."

Adam was listening, but only with one part of his

brain. Another was constructing a list of lies and pleas to deploy on Colegrave to buy his silence. And another was looking for weapons. His blocks of training and discipline, variously incomplete and specialized, were a gang of bastards ranged around the back of his skull and shouting orders over each other.

"I don't know anyone here," Adam said. "Only Clough and Lela Charron. And I don't really know even them, it's just that they're the only people who've talked to me."

"Have you had a proper look around yet? Taken a pass at recognizing or engaging anyone?"

"No. I got here yesterday, they doped me and put me to bed, I was woken by the staff banging on Mansfield's door, everything's happened at fucking once."

"Then you need to go for a walk. See who you can see. Gather allies. Fellow detectives. You have all the resources, Dearden. You shall be our agent in Normal. Do you accept?"

All the voices in Adam's head went silent. The walls warped a little, and his perception of perspective got a little dented. The strain of the interview may have been burning his meds faster, he supposed. But he'd said it. He'd had that instinct that something was wrong beyond the details of the abduction himself, and that something needed to be done. He couldn't lie to himself again. Lying to himself had probably taken him halfway to needing to be sent to Normal.

"Yeah. Yeah, I do."

Colegrave clapped his hands together. They made a noise like dry timbers. "Bravo. Now. Tell me everything you remember about the aftermath of the abduction that you saw. Every detail. Asher! Bring us two bottles of chilled Buoylent. The Carrot and Apple Surprise flavor, if you can." Colegrave raised one eyebrow at Adam. "The Surprise is that it's never seen a carrot or an apple in its brief laboratory life. I happen to like the flavor because it is precisely the kind of cheap chemical slurry that will sustain the existence of the peasant class in the world to come. It's strange, Dearden. We live in such a debased time, and yet we can quite literally taste the future. You have to admit that that's kind of wonderful."

Colegrave was beaming. His teeth were tiny and square with precisely even spacing between them and all the hues of rust and moss that an abandoned shack in the woods could attain, a grotesque display of nature's comedy dentistry assembled at micrometer tolerances.

They became almost companionable over their bottles of fluorescent orange Buoylent mix—of a shade, Colegrave noted approvingly, that did not occur in nature—and the recitation of the night's events. Colegrave asked intelligent questions, and Adam became aware that he was in fact in the presence of an intellect, no matter how corroded on its surface. Colegrave seemed to enjoy having a novel problem to solve, and worked without a notebook or other aide-mémoire. Adam would sometimes see Colegrave's eyeballs jitter around in his head as if he were in REM sleep with his lids up, and decided that the older man was meticulously arranging the components of Adam's report upon the shelves and in the trunks of a vast and doubtlessly richly Gothic memory palace.

When they were done—and focusing on details had allowed Adam to mentally even out a little, into something like comfort—Adam felt emboldened enough to ask Colegrave about the future he kept alluding to, hoping to learn something about the man's work.

Colegrave wriggled in his chair with pleasure. "Ah. The great epiphany, Dearden. Let me start here. Would you agree that all the major societies of this Earth are broken? Those things that we call civilizations? Are they all busted and terrible systems?"

"It's hard to argue with," Adam said.

"Yes, it is. And so many people in our field start looking for forward escape. Pushing through the current terrors and into a place where things start working again. This is why a lot of us devolved to singularitarianism, the notion of a technological critical mass that would produce artificial superintelligences that would, in a nutshell, fix everything. That notion in itself leads to what's called a singleton condition: the entirety of the world under a single command structure that is utterly impervious to any form of threat. A singleton could also be attained by a totalitarian human global government with flawless fine-grained surveillance methods and perfected psychological combat affordance.

"But!" Colegrave beamed, raising just one blade of a finger. "Given that artificial intelligence and world governments are unlikely in the extreme, this would seem to be a dead end, wouldn't it? So we do nothing. We are futurists. We look forward. Here is the revelation, Dearden. We had almost exactly such a thing, a long time ago. Back in the days when our worlds were smaller and crossing them was a lifetime's work. We had single units of governance that guided and controlled our lives with absolute power. Until we went mad, and the madness crawled through the structures of the world and brought us to our current lunatic impasse. The future, Dearden, is in fact a return to feudal monarchy. Proper hierarchical governance. An archaic revival, on the unassailable basis that democracy turns everything to shit and our accretion of freedoms has been entirely worthless if not completely toxic to our happiness and well-being. We need a Restoration."

"A restoration of what? There are still monarchies."

"Pale ghosts of what they were. Look. Monarchies and aristocracies worked for a very, very long time. The weight of the evidence of history is with them, not with the project of democracy or even communism, which commits the same sin of being by definition a government of the 'people.' The last five hundred years constitute a horror story wherein the villains of the piece stole power from a stable governance system in order to cast the population of the world into an ongoing lab experiment with no plan or boundary. A dismal science. Can you even imagine the way we live now being tolerated in city-states and kingdoms of the past? God, no. The near future is the resurgence of deep history. It is very beautiful."

Colegrave grinned. His gums were bleeding.

"I don't really want outsiders asking me awkward questions, either."

PART THREE

fter so long trapped in the micro-home with Colegrave, leaving the capsule felt like being ejected into space. Asher had conveniently vanished, so Adam was left without a copilot for the fall back to the main compound.

Adam didn't feel in great shape. The lengthy inquisition by Colegrave had burned through his deposits of useful body chemicals and sugars, it felt. It had, he admitted to himself, often been an entertaining experience, but now his tanks were empty and he needed either fuel or airplane mode. Being slumped in a seat, unable to communicate and watching the world rush by through a window, sounded very good to him.

Adam took some steps away from the micro-home and looked around, both to confirm his bearings and to take in the woodland, which was becoming more beautiful to him. Even the smells. He tended to personally dismiss "nature" as stuff that mostly rots and leaks, even as he made the right noises and faces to environmentalists and geoengineers. Maybe, he thought, everything was just cleaner out here, and so he could more easily detect the pure notes of forest scent. Maybe this was what they were talking about, all along.

Adam stood there and wondered what it would be like to live at Normal Head forever, like Colegrave. Would it feel like being trapped? Or would it feel like being free? There was a lot of space. There was a forest. There was so much silence. The quiet felt like a huge new country that he could wander around within for years without ever meeting its coastlines. A silence the size of the sky. If he stayed here long enough, he'd eventually be sent to Staging, and he'd have one of these simple, clever micro-homes to live and work in. There would be internet, and books, and music. He could think, and be, and hold the world at a distance in order to see it properly. Nothing would ever hurt or frighten him again. The micro-home of his very own could be his hermit's cave. He could be a wise man of the woods, spoken of in whispers, his words and thoughts becoming spooky action at a distance in the world beyond. A secret wizard of the future.

Adam was pleased by the idea. He was pleased that

he could be pleased by something again. He found an old smile from some deep dark pocket, and put it on. He took a deep breath of the treeline air. There was human sweat in it, sharp and acid.

There was a figure behind the treeline, just east of Colegrave's house.

An Indian woman, barefoot, hair tied back with a long weed-vine freshly yanked out of the ground. Her skin was smeared in moss, and her feet were caked in mud. She wore a sports bra that may historically have been white and the ugliest knee-length shorts in the world. She fixed him with a gaze that said that she had looked into the void and that she was really not impressed with it.

Adam sketched a pathetic little wave that he regretted attempting even as he was doing it.

"We are Jasmin Bulat," she said. "What are you?"

"Adam Dearden."

She cocked her head in an unusual way that seemed to Adam as if she was trying to help something else inside her skull get a look at him through her eyes.

"We know that name."

Adam walked around, trying to get a better angle on her and whoever was accompanying her.

There didn't seem to be anybody with her.

"How do you know my name?"

"We're not sure," Bulat said, picking a clump of moss off the side of her shorts. "It will come to us. Why were you talking to Colegrave?"

"Does it matter?"

"Very much so," she said, popping the piece of moss into her mouth and chewing meditatively. "Colegrave is quite, quite mad. Walk with us."

Adam remembered something Clough had said. Colegrave and Bulat. Adam summoned up whatever fumes were left in his tank and decided that, having already experienced Colegrave, he might as well collect the set. He followed her, and she turned and strolled back into the forest.

"Colegrave will never leave Normal Head," she said. "Not for the reasons he told you, of course. We doubt anyone with two brain cells to rub together is genuinely frightened of his berserk political fantasies. In some ways, he's very clever, but his understanding of the way the world really works—or, perhaps, just his perception of it—is hopelessly damaged. It's a pity. And we mean 'pity' on several different levels, because it's also quite pathetic. Adam Dearden. We do know that name."

Adam was enjoying the soft crunch of the forest floor underfoot, that few millimeters of travel it had as he took each step.

"We," Bulat said, "are the senior unit in Staging."

"Colegrave told me he was the senior figure."

"We have the higher qualifications in the outside world. Also, Colegrave is a foresight strategist, as you are. We are a strategic forecaster. As you once were. This is a natural advantage. Hence, we are the senior figure."

Adam considered the possibility that shoelessness was a sign of rank in Staging. "Colegrave told me that the demarcation doesn't exist in Staging."

In the next moment, he realized she had remembered his name.

"Demarcations exist everywhere. Does Colegrave know you crossed the aisle?"

She looked over her shoulder at him. He didn't feel like lying to the woman with the blazing eyes.

"He does," Adam said, "but he doesn't know all the details."

"We are very good at storing memories," Bulat said, patting her stomach as if to indicate that she kept extra memory there.

"What do you know about me?"

"We remember a private presentation or two about psyops. We imagine the business overnight with that Mansfield was very interesting to you, as it was to many on our side of the aisle."

Adam jogged to catch up with her. Somehow she always remained three steps ahead of him. "Why do you keep saying 'we'?"

"Because there is more than one sapient entity within this skin, of course. Are you an idiot?"

"No."

"We think you might be. We think you have never really listened to your internal voices. How can you never have heard their call? Only idiots are so insensible to the true sound of the body. Your voices are likely starved, anyway." She looked him up and down, critically. "You don't spend much time in nature."

"I can operate shoes," Adam said. "And I may be messed up right now, but I'm not hearing voices in my head, nor am I eating lichen."

She stopped, pivoted stickily on one heel, and confronted him. She pointed to her belly once more. "Not in your head. In here. You're just like the others. You cannot hear the biome."

All at once, Adam knew exactly why Jasmin Bulat was at Normal Head.

"You say 'we,'" Adam said, "because you count your gut microbiota as a second person inside you."

"The Buoylent is terrible for us. We have to augment our diet in the forest, because materials in that laboratory slurry kill parts of us. And the biome is really much, much more than just a voice. What if we told you that the biome is speaking to you now?"

Adam just smiled, closemouthed, to communicate that he was trying to be polite.

Bulat cast her eyes around the forest floor, and delightedly alighted upon an ant climbing a stalk of weed.

"The ant," she said. "Particularly susceptible to a species of mushroom called *Cordyceps*. It will grow in the brain of an ant. It will, in fact, induce an ant to scale a plant and keep it there like a tiny, triumphant mountaineer until it dies. After death, the mushroom will expand, push through and explode the ant's head. At this increased altitude, the mushroom can cast its spores a far greater distance than on the ground. The mushroom speaks to the ant. It has been doing so for almost fifty million years. And then, and for the last five hundred years or more, the *Cordyceps* is harvested, processed, and introduced into human bodies for medicinal purposes and, more recently, athletic enhancement. A voice that makes us climb faster."

"That's a far cry from telling me your gut bacteria talks to you."

"Some ninety percent of this body is bacteria. Yours, too. Gut biome connects directly to the enteric nervous system, which runs a hundred million neurons that connect directly to the central nervous system, and controls most of the body's supply of serotonin, the neurotransmitter that operates memory and learning. And all this is commanded by the biome. The gut records. The gut knows. Gut instinct? We always understood. We always knew that we just had to listen to the biome."

Adam watched the ant crest the top of the weed, and begin crawling back down the other side.

"Listen to your gut, Adam Dearden. What do you think happened last night?"

Adam looked around, mostly just to make sure he still knew where he was in relation to the main building, but also to buy himself a moment to decide what to say. To decide how much to trust this woman who was out in the forest trying to be a better host for her intestinal flora.

"I think it was a prank," he said. "Or it was a psychological operation."

"Tell me how you came to this."

"Nothing else makes a lot of sense to me. It's too . . . detailed. Too tailored. A couple of hundred pounds of bugs swapped for a man in the middle of the night? That's some seriously bored long-term patients. Or some seriously neurodivergent people on the wrong meds. It's something that crazy people might do. Not beyond the realm of possibility, right?"

"Or?"

"Or Normal Head has been targeted for a massively destabilizing psyop targeted specifically for the nature and condition of the audience. Depending on where your head is at, it's either a ridiculous thing that speaks to the ease with which someone can bypass security here, or it's a hallucinatory image designed to freak out fragile and paranoid people. The question there is why. A stunt's only intent is to amuse the instigators. And piss off a bunch of your fellow inmates, I suppose. A psyop needs a reason. Somebody would have to benefit from destabilizing a rest home full of sick futurists."

"'The audience.' You are one of us, aren't you?"

Adam had slipped. "The Audience" was how people working in psyops habitually referred to the witnesses and targets of operations.

She smiled at him for the first time. "Your secret is safe with us. Walk with us some more. We had a deal of engagement with psyops, back when we were outside, but it wasn't really our particular field. Aah. Back when we were outside."

"You sound like you miss it."

"Is that surprising?"

"Maybe a little. Colegrave obviously likes it here."

"We think we mentioned to you that Colegrave is mad."

"I don't want to be rude, but you're in Staging, and the way you behave kind of indicates that you have no great urge to leave."

Bulat smiled again, but it was sadder this time. "We do. It's just that we can't. We hope we might, someday. But, you see, the connection between the meat brain and the gut brain that we have worked so hard to open is still imperfect. The biome also regulates things like anxiety, you see, and the more traffic we put through the connection, the more disruption occurs to our system as a side effect."

"You get depressed."

"We get depressed. We gaze into our own internal abyss, and we see only struggle and pain and the barest hope of a perfect solution in our future. Just like everybody else here. We're often no different, in Staging. For a lot of us, Staging is as much of the outside world as we dare to engage with. If we leave now, we run the risk of not functioning in situations that are not safe. Have you ever been to Kazakhstan?"

"I did a conference in Astana once," Adam said.

"You should have traveled," Bulat said, quietly. "Our mother is from Mumbai, but our father is Kazakh, from Almaty. The landscapes are incredible. Steppe and grassland, snowy mountains and deep canyons, deltas and forest. The Oregon forest sometimes reminds us of the taiga, a little bit. All the fir trees. The Baikonur Cosmodrome is in Kazakhstan. Russia leases the land, but you can go there, if you know the right people. Where Yuri Gagarin was launched into space. They still call the launchpad he was fired from 'Gagarin's Start.' Valentina Tereshkova. The Mir space station. We saw things hurled into space from there and thought that space was the future. By the end of our time in the outside world, we were trying to convince militaries and states to grow spacecraft, with thick walls of rich ecologies, to support our gut biomes. Otherwise, space was pointless. We couldn't maintain our operating partners on probiotic yogurt and food paste. We cannot go to space and continue to hear our inner voice. We were trapped in the world long before we were taken to Normal Head."

Bulat blinked heavily a few times, and then just said, in a low voice, "You should have seen more of the countryside." She took a deep, shaky breath, and added, "What do you think will happen when the investigators get here?"

"I think," Adam said, "that I will be the first person they question."

"Because you arrived the day before it happened. Colegrave must have commented on that."

"He did, but he didn't seriously entertain the idea that I was involved. He said that I was the best person to start a drive to look at the thing ourselves, because I've worked on both sides."

"Colegrave didn't suggest that you might have an especial reason to want to solve the problem yourself?"

Adam took a new look at her. She was a lot more engaged than she'd seemed to him on first meeting, and that may have been due more to an unfair reading of the woman on his part than any fault of hers. "He didn't get that far. But you're thinking that I might have reasons to not want to be closely questioned by outside investigators."

"We think you might want to get ahead of whatever happens next. We also think that Normal Head is our home for the foreseeable future and we would prefer it not become part of the global combat theater. If there is anywhere in the world that should not be just another trench in the permanent condition of pervasive low-level warfare, it should be here."

"I don't think this place has any more right to peace than, say, a hospital. Which it pretty much is."

"It is a hospital, but it has only one kind of patient. People who have tried to look into the future in order to try to save the world and have been driven insane by it. The worst kind of insanity, Adam Dearden. We've all been sent mad by grief."

Special pleading for crazy futurists. Adam worked hard to keep his opinion from showing on his face. Looking up and away because he didn't trust himself to meet Bulat's eyes and not laugh, he found that she had led them around to the treeline again, fifty yards down from the point where he'd entered the forest. He could see the side entrance to the main building.

"There," she said. "Home again. We are going back into the forest for a few more hours, to replenish ourselves and listen to the biome of the woods. You should go to work. Before people come to ask you questions that you really don't want to answer."

Jasmin Bulat squelched back into the cool, welcoming shade of the forest, leaving him to face the concrete and glass.

Adam almost twisted his ankle on the way through the door, by trying not to tread on some fat weevil thing, which was also the point where Adam admitted to himself that he knew pretty much nothing about nature because he was taxonomizing insects as "weevil thing." Which gave him some cause for concern that he was more like Colegrave than like Bulat, whom he found far warmer and more human even though she thought she was in a symbiotic relationship with her gut bacteria. Though it was a further cause for concern that both of them seemingly did work that was sent from and transmitted to the outside world, where it was presumably used for real things that could affect people.

Work that was now disrupted because the internet connection in Staging was switched off.

The thought stopped him in the corridor as it came into focus. He was getting foggy enough that he didn't know if he'd fully understood the idea before, but it was there now, as clear as the fat weevil that had tried to kill him by predating on his wish not to crush fat weevils that didn't deserve crushing.

What if it was an operation intended to cut Normal Head off and subject it to a higher than normal level of scrutiny? Obviously there was a protocol in place for anomalous events, and the Director enacted it. Decapitating the place from the body of the world, which means that work no longer flowed into or out from Staging. Something that would have occurred very early on to brains less addled than his. Which was partly because, Adam also had to admit to himself, he was more concerned by being forced to answer questions asked by complete strangers with an investigational remit, questions and answers that wouldn't be covered under doctor/patient privilege.

"Oh, fuck," he said, and sat down in the middle of the corridor and held his head in his hands.

Dickson appeared from nowhere like the world's shittiest elf, sweating, bloodshot eyes on stalks and grinding his teeth like he was trying to gnaw through a railroad track. "What's up? What's up? What's up?"

Adam looked up at Dickson with tears in his eyes. "Could I have lunch? Lunch is a thing I used to have. I would really like lunch."

———

Out on the patio again, Dickson's friendly hand on Adam's upper arm, threading him between the tables and holding him up when his knees threatened to fold. Lela spotted him, and, getting up from his own table, so did Clough. Adam saw Lela sigh and then haul herself from her chair grudgingly, preparing to try to score some more social points to get her into Staging. Clough's table was close to the gap between strategic forecast and foresight strategy. Adam indicated to Dickson that they should head toward Clough. Lela watched them change tack and followed.

Clough stretched a big spade of a hand out. "All right, lad?"

Adam took Clough's wrist, and looked over on the other side. He saw a table with only one person seated at it. "Take me over there, Dickson. Clough's coming too."

"Okay," said Dickson, doubtfully. Adam looked over his shoulder at Lela. "Come on," he said.

"Let go," Clough said.

"Do what I say or the *Danger Mouse* DVD is history," Adam said.

"You heartless fucking bastard."

They crossed the aisle, from foresight strategy to strategic forecast.

The entire space went deathly silent.

Hundreds of eyes on them as they moved to that table with just one person at it. Adam sat down opposite that person, and looked with intent at Clough. Clough sat down like a dying man giving up the ghost and dropping into his own coffin. Lela stood a few feet away, stranded in their wake.

Adam cast his eyes up to Dickson and said, "Thank you. Am I allowed food I can chew? I'd really like to try some food, if that's okay?"

"Sure it is, Mr. Dearden. I'll go check and see what I can find for you. Are you going to be okay here?"

"I'm fine," Adam said. Dickson had the demeanor of a man watching an insane person urinating in a christening bowl and being unable to do anything meaningful about it. He shook his head and left at an amphetamine trot.

The person in front of Adam was a rheumy-eyed man in a pointed woolen pom-pom hat with considerable earflaps. He clutched a steaming cup of what looked and smelled like hot berry juice between hands wearing both Thinsulate gloves and knitted shooting mittens, the top halves of them folded back so he could use his fingers. There were so many layers of knitwear on the man that Adam could not easily estimate his actual size.

Adam dropped everything he was planning to recite and just said, "Are you okay?"

"Do I look okay?" A little bit of Jamaica in his accent.

"Well . . . not really? But it's not that cold."

"A black man can't live like this. It's too far north.

Did you know there are only nine black people in Canada? I counted."

"I think that's a made-up number."

"It is a made-up number, but I counted it, so it's true. You are on the wrong side of the aisle, pale frost creature asshole."

"My name's Adam Dearden."

"I know your kind have names. Didn't ask to know what they were. Snow-colored mutant fuck."

Adam went to speak, and then swallowed back the words, looked at Clough, took a moment to reconfigure his approach.

"Okay," Adam resumed. "What do you think happened to that Mansfield guy, and what are we going to do about it?"

"Son," the man in the hat said, "you came from the wrong side of the aisle, so I can't even hear you. You scuttle on back to The Shire there and leave the grown-ups alone."

"It is, at worst, fifty-five degrees out here. I know what side of the goddamned aisle I walked over here from. How about you stop playing children's games and tell me what you're so afraid of?"

The man's eyebrows ascended into his hat. "Afraid?"

"You're sitting here clutching a hot drink and all hunched up like you think the boogeyman is going to appear from nowhere and cup your balls. You're all sitting here in terrified silence," Adam continued, raising his voice, "worried to all hell that people are going to come and ask you awkward questions. Or that people are going to come and take you away in the night. Or that you've pissed off someone somewhere who just wanted to come in and scare the shit out of you to let you know they know who and where you are. Am I getting warm yet, Nanook of the fucking North? How about the rest of you?"

The man in the hat pulled his right hand from his drink and shook one trembling finger at Adam, the cap of the shooting mitten wobbling comically under it. "My name, you fucking northern cave gimp, is Darnel Booth, and it is nowhere near fifty-five degrees, and your incredible lack of manners is forgiven only by the fact that you do not come from a civilized part of the world that was actually intended to support human life."

"You're Darnel Booth? What the hell happened to you?"

"Hey. You don't look like an Olympic athlete yourself, and we're both in Normal Head, so how about a bit more respect?"

"Darnel Booth." Adam turned to Clough. "Darnel *Booth. Negation Risk Scenario Planning.*"

"I never saw that film," Clough said.

"It wasn't a . . . Christ. I thought you worked in economic foresight?"

"Well, I do, but it's like I told you. I mostly get bankers and politicians drunk."

"Don't do this," Darnel muttered.

"*Negation Risk*," Adam continued. "The first modern study to identify the issues around scenarios other than nuclear war that would wipe out all trace of human civilization as if we were never here. It was groundbreaking."

"And you're asking what happened to him?" Clough chuckled.

"Oh," Adam said. "Right."

"I'm not depressed," Darnel said, hands back around his hot drink. "I just came to a natural conclusion. We should have stayed in Africa. Africa is the environment we evolved for. Technically speaking, it is the only inhabitable part of the world. The only way we will survive into the future is if we fortify the cradle of humanity and fend off you ghost-walkers with heavy armaments. I'm okay with the Indians and Chinese. But they can't come in. The only mistake I made was writing that paper."

"You haven't published in three years," Adam said.

"I was consulting for DARPA. Probably sending it over to them was a mistake. They never released it. I protested. Some people might have gotten hurt. There may have been construction work. Possibly a small bomb. So here I am."

Darnel Booth met Adam's eyes, just once. "Maybe a little bit of abyss gaze," Darnel said.

A Nordic blonde woman, six feet tall and perhaps forty, loomed over the end of the table. "You are the Stoop Model man."

Adam's stomach fell away.

"You are. I remember you. The Washington Unmanned Airspace conference. I slept with your friend from Kolkata. You have not gotten more attractive during the intervening years."

"Nanfrid Skoglund," Adam said.

"You remember!"

"Not an easy name to forget," Adam said.

"You are the Stoop Model man. Do you have an email address for your friend from Kolkata?"

"Sorry."

Nanfrid turned to address people at the next table over. "This is the Stoop Model guy! You remember that? He has a funny face still."

"Do I have a funny face?" Adam asked Clough.

"Everyone looks a bit Cubist to me, these days, to be honest," Clough said. "I'm not sure where your nose is supposed to be."

"I thought I saw you," said a smaller and much slimmer woman, pulling herself upright from the other table. "Adam, right? You did a bunch of warfighter theory at

FortStrat back in the day. Stoop Model and other stuff. Stoop was a hell of a thing."

A quiet voice behind Adam said, "What's this Stoop thing?" It was Lela, who'd been standing just outside Adam's peripheral vision the whole time he'd been seated. Adam thought she'd drifted loose and fallen back to the other side of the patio.

"Stoop Model. Right. I'm Morelia, by the way. Morelia Gorski. Nice to meet you. Nice to meet you too. And you. I've met you, Darnel, don't look at me like that. This was back in the early days of serious thinking about drones for warfighting, right? We had, like, Predator drones, and Reaper drones, and things like that, and the military and political clients were pushing all of us hard for urban drone solutions. But you can't just stick a flight of Predator drones into a city, especially a vertical Western city, you know?"

"Why would you even want to do that?" Lela asked.

"Eh," Morelia shrugged. "Crowd control. Riot management. Disrupting occupations. Like that. So, anyway, everyone's getting pushed to come up with urban solutions for these big honking drones. And, remember, these things are thirty feet long with fifty-foot wingspans. They ain't like flying your little quadcopter you got from Amazon for your birthday, but you can't hang fourteen missiles off a quadcopter. And Adam here, he saw years ahead. Adam, did you see somebody's doing a Kickstarter for micro-drones you can launch off your wrist like a bird of prey now?"

"No," Adam lied.

"See, that was Adam's thing. Birds of prey. Birds of prey, they circle around their target, way high above, and when they're ready, they just drop at high speed to hit their target with total precision. And that's called a stoop, see? Adam saw that you didn't need a big honking drone. You just needed a flight of lots of little micro-drones built around chunks of explosive material. So, say you were trying to control a riot that had a dozen ringleaders. You could stoop-kill just those twelve people, without harming anyone else. Smack 'em in the head with a micro-drone carrying enough of an explosive core to blow their brains out. Stoop Model decapitation strikes. It was brilliant, really. The only problem was effectively guiding them in, because you need really fine-grained oversight of the theater of action and lots and lots of live take and real-time processing. But the theory took everybody off in a whole new direction. Brilliant, man. Brilliant."

Adam could feel Lela's eyes boring into the back of his neck like he had revealed a swastika tattoo there.

"And now," Morelia continued blithely, "like I say, people are designing wrist-launched drones. Just like a falconer releasing a bird off his glove. You saw the future, man. You're one of the real few, you know? You saw the actual manufactured future."

Darnel raised his fist to Adam for a bump, and somberly intoned, "Smart shit, man. That was some smart shit."

Adam tapped his fist to Darnel's, and heard the Thinsulate crinkle. Darnel pulled his hand away slowly and splayed his fingers. Exploding fistbump. "Steely-eyed missile man," Darnel said.

"Are you sure you don't have your friend's email address?" Nanfrid said. "He had a very strange penis, and it made me like women more, but every now and then I like to check. Also he would make a very interesting medical study for when they let me out. Please tell no one. My medical studies are why I'm here. Your genetics must be awful. Did your mother like the zoo more than she should have when you were a child? Did she spend a lot of time there alone?"

"You should excuse Nanfrid," Morelia said. "She should probably be in prison."

Clough was regarding Adam stonily. "So your job was working out how to blow protesters' heads off? Fuck me."

"And he's awesome at it. On paper, I mean," Morelia said.

"Morry," Darnel said quietly, considering the last of the juice in his cup. "He walked over from the other side of the aisle."

"Oh, wow," Morelia said. "So that's where you went. You got a case of the touchy-feelies and went to the other side?"

"Wouldn't have put it quite like that," Adam mumbled.

"It's okay, Adam. Not everybody's cut out for having a real job and defending the future from the forces of darkness."

"Oh, fuck you," Lela said.

Very mildly, Morelia responded with a simple "Fuck you back. I'm guessing you're from the land of hugs and bunnies too?"

"I'm from the land of helping make sure living in a city doesn't kill you while you sit in a room in a city devising ways to kill people."

"That's awfully sweet. You have fun with that while I work with a team to arrange water security so you're not drinking out of ditches while drawing your little maps."

Darnel drained his cup, eyes softly closed, as if he were miles away in a peaceful field.

"My maps are how clean water gets to your death bunker and has been since people in cities started thinking about how people—"

Clough stirred to life. "None of you know shit about shit. Money. Money is what pays for us all to be here. Money drives your life, and yours," he said, pointing at Morelia and Lela in turn, "and every other bloody thing.

We are all just greedy fucking monkeys playing with dirt and bones in the shadow of money. Money's the thing we made that owns us. You're both wrong and you should both shut up. I'm being held hostage here by the only currency that matters here now, which is *Danger Mouse.*"

A broad man wearing three T-shirts, each of which was made for men of different shapes from his, hove into the conversation, bumping into the table. He had trouble moving his legs and his skin was ripe with broken veins. "Money doesn't own us. The only thing that will own us like that is strong artificial intelligence. Money will just cause it. That's what you should be worrying about. Idiots with all the money, plowing it into building a thing just because they can. My name is Gaige. I would shake hands, but I fear nanotechnological contamination. I prefer to keep an airgap, you see."

"There's no such thing as 'nanotechnological contamination,'" Darnel observed, in a mild voice.

"And you know everything, do you?" Gaige asked. "You know precisely what's being developed and tested in skunkworks and black labs all over the world?"

A few more people washed up around their table.

"I kind of invented the modern end of the world, pal," Darnel offered.

"No, you didn't," Clough said. "Money. Whatever prehistoric goat-fiddler invented money invented the end of the world. Only the Romans understood what happened. They knew we created a thing like a god, and they gave it a name and a fucking temple. Juno Moneta, mate. 'Moneta' from '*moneres*,' which is Latin for fucking warning. They said it."

"We're kind of getting off the subject I was wanting to explore here," Adam said. But Clough appeared to have found himself a plastic pulpit there at the table.

"Money," Clough declaimed, "is the dark unknown god driving us all towards certain bloody doom. A giant formless thing from beyond space with a million genitals. It's the thing in the horror films that you should not directly look at lest you go mad and all that bollocks. It's crushed the world into new shapes and all we want to do is drink its dark milk because that is the nature of its horrible fucking magic. It's why we're all here. And whatever happened to Mansfield is about money. And all the things they're going to come and ask you are all about money. Who profits from what happened last night? And why don't you care?"

Voices were raised, disagreeing.

"Well, if you are all so terribly bloody concerned," laughed Clough, "why aren't you talking about it?"

Arguments burst across the patio like fireworks.

Clough patted Adam on the shoulder. "There you go, lad. Bring me my *Danger Mouse* and all is forgiven and forgotten. *Danger Mouse* is the only god I have now."

Adam looked around. Slowly, steadily, the line between the two sides was being erased by a rolling conversation. In some places, impassioned debate. In others, low-voiced serious discussion with people describing shapes and angles on tabletops with their fingers.

Even at his own table, wild statements and crazy manifestos were cooking down into forensic explorations of who actually benefited from making a man disappear. They were engaged. Not, Adam realized, engaged with the painful textures of the real, outside world, but with the smaller, more manageable little world of Normal.

Adam became aware of something at his elbow. He jerked his arm up, instinctively acting as if Dickson was behind him, touching that elbow to guide him away. He wasn't done, and wasn't going anywhere. But Dickson wasn't there. That tiny weight, that sense of presence, was one of those fat bugs. A weevil or a roach or whatever the hell you call them. The tubby little bastard had crawled up the chair and onto his elbow. Adam waved his arm about, trying to shake it off, but it was hanging on. The thing was awkward to get to. Adam was, absurdly, reminded that no healthy human had ever touched their right elbow with their right hand. It was scuttling around his upper arm, and the problem, Adam admitted, was that he didn't want to touch the damned thing with his bare fingers.

He found the ridiculous courage to pluck the bug off. He tossed it onto the table, picked up Darnel's empty cup, and used it as a ram to crush the crawling annoyance. It made a surprisingly satisfying crack.

Everyone around the table stared at him, and Adam realized that he might have vocalized something in the region of a somewhat gladiatorial "*Ha*" as he'd done it.

"What?" Adam said. "I've been dodging these fucking bugs and weevils and roaches all day. It's not like we're in a Buddhist temple. I'm a pursuit predator at the top of the food chain and this is a fucking insect that was annoying me. I've got too much else going on to feel guilty about it, so stop looking at me like that."

Adam looked down at the smashed bug.

"Oh, shit," he said.

PART FOUR

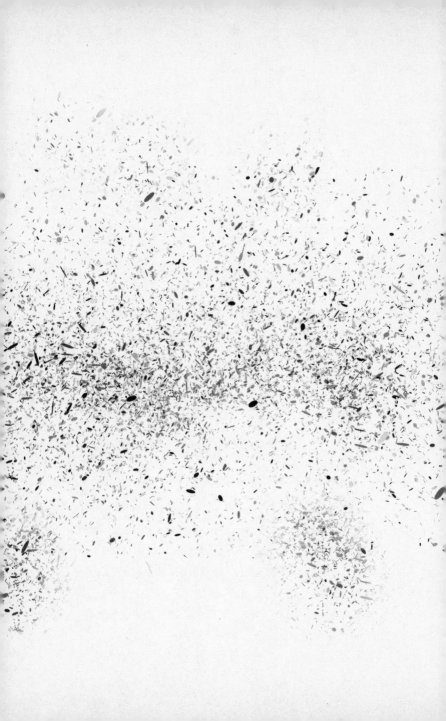

Well, would you look at that," Darnel said.

The fat insect had cracked open. But it hadn't cracked open in the way a fat insect would. It had split and shattered the way a dropped cell phone might. Its carapace had starred like windshield glass around the split. There was nothing wet inside it. Nothing organic.

Adam was looking at wires. Wires and tiny electronic devices and mechanics. Radio antennae. Shrunken microphones. Something that might be a memory card. A cluster of litter processors. Glassine dust that may once have belonged to a lens. He was looking at a device in the shape of a fat insect.

Lela leaned over Darnel's shoulder. "Jesus fucking

Christ. Where did this come from? Those look like tiny, tiny KERS systems."

"I dunno what that is," said Darnel, "but I'm pretty sure this here is a microphone."

"KERS. Kinetic energy recovery system. We've been testing all kinds of versions in cities for generating electricity from people walking on sidewalks. This is just a totally miniaturized version, you can tell by that armature. This thing makes its own energy by walking. I mean, it'd run down in the end, but it could have months before you'd have to plug it into something."

"I ain't looking for the USB port on this thing."

Adam sat back and scoured his recent memory. Insect in the hallway. Insect on the skirting board. Spider in Dr. Murgu's office. Spider in Dr. Murgu's office that was not spinning a web in the corner. There was no web anywhere. Just the spider.

Churning mass of insects on Mansfield's bed. And no Mansfield to be seen.

The tide of adrenaline almost blinded him.

Adam stood up, looked around quickly. A recently opened bottle of Buoylent on an adjacent table, its owner reaching for it. Adam lunged over, snatched it away, and sank it in one pull. Gasping, ignoring the complaints, he lurched to the next table, found an unopened bottle and did the same. If Buoylent really was loaded with mood stabilizers, he was going to need as many in his system as possible.

He clambered up on the table. Eyes came to rest on him from both sides of the patio.

"We," he said, in as loud and steady a voice as he could muster, "are going to have to find every single insect, bug, and crawly bastard in this place and smash it. If you want to know why, look over there. Lela Charron and Darnel Booth—one from each side of the aisle—are right now looking at an insect I crushed. It's got microphones in it. I bet you anything you like that it's also got radio. It's a listening device. And there could be more. A lot more. Like a couple of hundred pounds more. We need to find them all, right now, before the investigators get here. Whatever you've said in the last twenty-four hours is inside these things, people. Total surveillance in a place that is supposed to be free of all surveillance. If we don't get them, then whatever you say and do from now until you leave is going to be recorded and sent to people we do not know. Doesn't matter what side of the aisle you're on today. I know damn well that doesn't sound like a good and healthy situation to any of you."

He took a breath, and then said, "People. You're not crazy if there really are robot insects listening to every word you say."

Someone said, "I fucking *told* you."

People across the patio started getting up and looking around at the ground. Adam heard a thump: a shoe
coming off and its heel striking. Human buzzing, figures
hunching and crouching. And then a cry: "Bloody hell!"

That was it. Everyone was up and hunting. Shoes
were coming off for weaponry, full water and Buoylent
bottles brandished as truncheons. A swarm of damaged
academics given full rein to declare war on the natural
world. There was shouting, swearing, a cascade of smack-
ing sounds, some hurried strident conversations, even
some crying, but it seemed to Adam, looking out over
his works, that the loudest sound was laughter.

"Shit!" A woman's voice jumped above the noise.
"That one was real! I've got bug guts in my eye." The
laughter got louder still.

Adam got down off the table, having spied a broad
roach-like object running for cover under his table.
Adam slipped off a shoe, got down on his hands and
knees, and galloped after the object, dispatching it with
a swift blow of the heel. It split and stopped moving. Adam
scooped it up, extricated himself from the table, and left
the patio with all speed.

Adam told himself that he had to work fast. He
wasn't going to keep it together forever. Memories and
deductions were clawing at the edges of his vision, mon-
sters on the other side of the wall trying to chew their
way through.

In the corridor, he almost ran straight into Dickson, carrying a tray with a plastic-domed plate of salad on it.

"We agreed on a lunch for you. Had to talk it over with the nutritionists and your doctor."

"I'll be right back for it. Thanks so much. Really appreciate it. It's a bit crazy out there right now, but don't worry, I'll be back to explain it shortly. Thanks."

Adam kept moving. Down the corridors, out the side door, across the grass, over the stepping stones. Asher was standing with his back to Colegrave's front door, masturbating absentmindedly, gazing blank-eyed at the grass. He only woke from his daze as Adam got within ten feet of him, and even then didn't put it away.

"Sorry," Asher said. "Helps with the stress, you know. Helps me think. I used to be very important once. It was just that, after a while, nobody could stand the way I thought about things. Probably not an outlandish story here, is it?"

"I need to speak to Colegrave."

"Colegrave is communing with the *tenebris anima*."

"I don't even know what that is."

"The dark wind, Adam Dearden. The grim impetus of deep history that looks out of his eyes and tells him what to do. He might be naked, so prepare yourself. It's been known."

Only at that moment did Asher seem to detect the

wind himself. He looked down. "Oops. Better pop the Asherino back in, eh? Haha."

Adam shouldered the man out of the way and opened Colegrave's front door.

Colegrave was, in fact, simply reclined in his chair and staring at the ceiling.

"Colegrave. I know what's happening."

"That was worryingly swift, Dearden. Are you sure?"

Adam showed him the crushed device in his hand.

Colegrave studied it from several angles before picking the thing up with the tips of his fingers. His eyes narrowed as he peered inside its split casing as best he could.

"Audio pickups," he muttered. "And that flat black wafer underneath appears to be a style of integrated solid-state drive. I would imagine it's capable of storing up to sixty-four gigs of audio. For those periods where— ah, yes, there it is—where it can't use this little wi-fi aerial to squirt out what it's hearing to a base station, or, perhaps, talk to a cell phone. It can just record and then upload to base when it comes back into some signal. Fascinating."

"This," Adam said, "is a piece of Mr. Mansfield. There are a lot of them. Most of the patients are smashing every insect on the patio area into shrapnel right now. Do you understand me, Colegrave?"

Colegrave met Adam's eyes. "I believe I do. I would

like to know the identities of the investigators that are on their way here, and who they serve. The many entities who commission research work from Normal Head will have a definite interest in these events. I shall require our internet privileges to be reinstated."

"If the internet connection's up, aren't we running the risk of these things connecting to it somehow?"

"That's the point. I want to know who is behind this breach. With everyone in Staging working at their computers, we can await the moment when any remaining devices connect to the system and call home. We can manage the security of the connection. We trace their connection request and the address they're trying to reach, and strip out all the information that follows—let the stamped addressed envelope go but keep the letter, discovering whom they're attempting to speak to. For this to work, however, the Director has to give us access to the postal system. He has to restore internet access to Staging."

Adam dropped the crushed device into Colegrave's hand and left.

Asher was still outside, hands in his pockets and looking heartsick.

"I have small relapses," Asher said, not looking at Adam's face. "I'm not crazy anymore. I just have small relapses. The stress. Everything today. It's just too much, and I can't do anything."

Adam had a feeling that he was looking at the real Asher. The deceitful tone, the curling smile, the whole unpleasant mien of the man was gone, and what was left was a man who was intelligent enough to be scared and to know that his illness had taken the tools to deal with it away from him.

Adam's heart rate was starting to race. He knew he was running out of time. He knew he shouldn't waste functional moments on something Asher probably wouldn't remember tomorrow.

Adam turned around. He saw Bulat standing at the treeline, in the shade.

Bulat nodded at him, just once, and then stepped back into the forest.

"It's Ben, right?" Adam said. "Ben Asher?"

"Yes," Asher whispered. "Yes, I was."

"I'm going to need your help with the next bit, Ben. I can't do what needs to be done without a good man from Staging."

"I haven't been a good man in a long time," Asher said. "I used to work in geoengineering theory. Trying to save the world from climate change. Being a good man didn't make a damn bit of difference."

"Today it will," Adam said, arranging a very straight face and a sympathetic steepling of his eyebrows.

An expression crept over Asher's face that was not unlike that of a lonely child being told that Santa had not in fact been strangled to death in an alley in New Orleans.

Out on the patio, piles of smashed insect-devices were being created on the tables. These people being who they were, the piles were separated by taxonomy: fake spiders here, fake lice there, fake roaches on another. Dickson and five other orderlies were standing around, bouncing up and down on the balls of their feet and looking nervous.

"I ate your lunch," Lela said, walking up to Adam. "Where have you been?"

"Talking to Colegrave."

"Oh my God. You've been in Staging. Already."

"Just visiting. And let me tell you now, you are plenty sane enough to be in Staging. In fact, Ben Asher here is going to put in a word for you with Colegrave, using my name. Aren't you, Ben?"

"Absolutely," Asher said, extending a hand and looking to Adam for approval. Adam glanced at Ben's hand, then caught his eye and gave a quick little shake of his head.

"Oh," said Asher. "Right. Anyway. Yes. Ben Asher."

"Lela Charron," Lela said, picking up on the silent exchange and wrapping her hands behind her back.

"Darnel," Adam called. "Got a minute?"

Darnel, who had been considering one of the piles from a distance, jogged over, arms wrapped around himself against the supposed cold. "What's up?"

"I kind of want three representatives for the next bit," Adam said, and gathered them all up like stray ducklings in his wings, ushering them toward Dickson and the other staffers.

"Dickson," Adam said. "We need to see the Director, right now."

"That's not going to happen today, Mr. Dearden," Dickson said. "I am sorry, really. But you're not the first people to ask to talk to him today. Everyone just needs to stay calm until help arrives."

"The help arriving might be the actual problem. All we're being told is that 'investigators' are coming. Some of us have problems with that. Well, that and what you can see in front of you."

"No one will tell us what you're all doing out here. It just looks like you've all gone to war on the insect kingdom."

"We need to talk to the Director. We need the internet turned on and we need to draw up some emergency plans. We need to get into the Director's office, and we need to do that now. This is a request from representatives from both sides of the aisle, and from Staging."

"I can see that. But I just can't help you."

Ben Asher drew himself to his full height, and his

old smile snaked back onto his lips as he said, "Dickson, we are geniuses. We can get into the med store anytime we want, and we do. If you ever want to see your Ritalin again, you will get your friends to help us."

The five other orderlies visibly and audibly clenched.

Adam and a section of the inmate populace were guided by Dickson and his jittery friends through the halls and corridors of the main building. Darnel kept pace with Adam.

"Did you just enact a coup d'état in a mental hospital?"

"Just a temporary realignment of management priorities," Adam said. "A pivot in the nature of the Area of Responsibility."

"Damn. You really have worked both sides of the aisle, haven't you?"

"Think there's space for me on the ramparts of your future fortress?"

"Hell, no," Darnel said, picking up his pace. "You're a fucking mutant."

The Director was not thrilled by a pack of actual lunatics invading his office, and said so, in terms that were not medically professional.

"We want internet and we want to know who's coming. Or for you to stop them if you can."

"The investigators are already on their way. Apparently some initial group was scrambled together out of L.A., San Francisco, and Richmond. They got into a van at PDX. Why would I want to stop them from coming? I want some answers to this ridiculous situation. And I'm the Director."

"Who's sending them?"

"Hell if I know," the Director said. "The board. I don't need to know. The moment this mess got referred to the board, it was taken out of my hands,"

Darnel, eyes narrowed, asked, "What exactly do you do here?"

"Me? I arrange for your backsides to be wiped every day, and I answer to a board, and the board is made up of any number of universities, institutes, NGOs, and God knows what else. It's one giant organism put together out of a swarm of smaller ones who all transmit a little bit of money, which we gather up and use to keep you people in food and drugs. I keep the cash coming in and you whackjobs from going out."

"Is Normal worth so much money to anybody that a team of investigators for some black-swan event at Normal would be on call and 'scrambled' to get here?" Lela asked. "I mean, given that you just said that this place is funded by a flock of entities who all kick in five bucks each."

"The same flock of entities," the Director said, "who funded all your research posts and endless parade of conferences and all your other crap. So the answer is evidently yes. *I don't need to know why*. It's all out of my control now. I have a lot of inmates who used to be high-value people before they lost their shit and were given to me to hose down and dose up. Half of whom are probably here because of you, Dearden. You think I don't read the patient files? You did some dark surveillance-culture shit before you became a people person."

"Shut up. We need the internet restored to Staging, and, if you really don't know who's coming, we need them checked for communications devices when they come in."

"You can have the internet," the Director said, "because it's just become less annoying to give it to you rather than withhold it. But if you think I'm going to lift a finger when those people come here to save me from your crazy asses, then you're crazy. Wait."

The Director started giggling at his own "joke."

Adam was fast losing the will to live. He turned and looked at the others, hands spread.

"We," said Lela, "are going to need some nets."

"What?"

"Ad hoc urban event solutions," Lela said. "Pull all the bedsheets. They won't let us have anything sharp, so we'll have to twist them up into thick lengths and then knot them into netting. We'll fill empty Buoylent bottles with stones from the treeline and tie them into the nets as weights. We throw the nets on these investigators when they arrive, tangle them up, and then swarm them and grab their phones and sit on the bastards until we find out where they're from and what's going on."

"You're very organized." Adam smiled.

"I feel useful. I feel like I can do things. It's good."

"What you've got in mind might slow down your transfer to Staging, Lela."

She laughed in his face. "Robot beetles, conspiracies, and a takeover of Normal? I'd trade six weeks at Staging for today in a second. This is the most fun I've had in years. This is," and she jabbed his nose with a finger, "the best day I can remember having since I was seventeen."

"What happened when you were seventeen?"

"I burned down my old school. Let's get to it."

Adam watched everyone move. Pulling bedsheets, winding them into soft rods, and knotting them into giant floppy geodesic domes. Academics' hands all grimy with soil from scraping pebbles into empty corn-plastic bottles still slimed with Buoylent residue. It was kind of wonderful to see these people work. Even the sickest among them found smiles as they, too, watched the industry from safe corners.

Elected spotters at the main doors heard the trucks coming before anyone could see them. The shout went down the corridors. Adam was very tired, and stood by the serving counter by the medical storeroom as people rushed by him, talking and laughing, many of them trying not to trip as they carried their makeshift nets to the door.

He heard tires on the driveway. Doors opening. A great whoop and a holler, and then it all got started.

The chaos outside sounded like a flock of tornadoes all touching the earth at once. Everyone in the building was throwing themselves outside into the storm. Adam had a sudden vision of lemmings dressed up like cliché Midwestern farmers, hurling themselves into a twister. Comedy cinema suicide. He chuckled a little as he sidled into the abandoned medical storeroom, lifting a part-drunk water bottle off the countertop on his way. It was a nice thought to end on. He closed the storeroom door behind him.

Bouncing the bottle between his hands, Adam scanned the shelves. He was shopping, he told himself. Nothing more important than browsing the aisles at a supermarket. Some of the names on the labels meant nothing to him. He picked up one or two, to discover they were trademarked terms for medications he knew by original or generic names. Nothing useful. Light sleeping pills here, levelers for bipolar disorder there. He stretched up on his tiptoes to peer at the highest shelves.

There it was. Something he'd heard and read of, in the same way one hears and reads of a great band who never plays your town. Adam reached out for the bottle and then sat on the floor with it and his stolen water, with his back to the door. He read the tiny print on the back of the bottle's label as if it were the sleeve notes to a rare vinyl album. Not, it occurred to him, that anyone really wrote sleeve notes anymore. He knew, from long website essays, that sleeve notes had pretty much gone away by the end of the eighties. Adam searched for the word to describe the nostalgia for things you never knew. He was sure there was one, and that he'd once known it. Nostalgia for a word you once knew. Adam chuckled again, and forced the childproof lid off the plastic canister of pills.

Saudade? No, but it was similar. Adam cast around in his memory as he shook some of the contents into his palm. Red capsules. Sleeve notes were an important thing, he decided. They came from a time when music had something to say, and was supposed to mean something. Even the meaningless and indecipherable stuff, like prog rock, had something to say about aesthetic and form. It was an intensely civilized thing, the provision of sleeve notes. What was wrong with him, that he'd thought it was okay to live in a world without sleeve notes?

Adam ate six of the capsules and washed them down with a slug of water. The water was a little warm, and the mouth of the bottle tasted faintly of lipstick.

When was the last time he'd tasted lipstick? Adam paused, bottles in his lap, to hunt for it for a moment. A year? Probably a couple of years. It was different for a while, when he changed jobs. The surge of enthusiasm, the sudden lightness of a new life had made him more willing to take small chances and engage with people. It had, he reflected, probably made him more fun to be around. For a short period. It had definitely been a couple of years. He hadn't noticed, it seemed. Maybe everyone else had. Maybe everyone else saw that he had the fog of the abyss around his shoulders and kept their distance, and he really was just the last one to see it.

That said, Adam acknowledged with a shrug and a wry smile, Nanfrid was also right. He just wasn't very attractive. He shook out and ate another six Seconal, drank them back with the water. He shyly traced his tongue over his lips afterward, to taste the lipstick again, with slow consciousness.

Sehnsucht. That was the word, wasn't it? Unusually short for a German compound word with a complex meaning. Nostalgia for a distant country to which we have never been, but which nonetheless may be home. An intense yearning for a comforting alien perfection. Lipstick traces with no owner. Adam turned the word over in his head, as the taste faded on his tongue. Another sad futurist, he thought, trying to summon an ideal world from its island moorings in tomorrow. Ridiculous way to live.

He wondered why he was eating the capsules six at a time. He knew from school that six was a perfect number, though he couldn't for the life of him remember why. He swallowed another six. It took two sips of water to get them down, this time. He supposed his body was getting sluggish. God knows it was more comfortable, sitting on the floor and leaning against the door, than it had any right to be. This was, he decided, really the most pleasant time he'd had since arriving in Normal Head. Possibly the most pleasant time he'd had this year. A quiet room. Nobody watching or listening. Adam could find it in himself to feel bad for the people outside this room. Nobody outside this room would ever again be alone in the way that he was alone in that moment. Nobody was ever going to be safe again. The tipping point had been found and operated. He didn't find that these conclusions were especially affecting his mood. They were just there.

Sitting there, he conceived of the notion that a good futurist should know when to quit. A good futurist should know when the game is over, and bail out. The game he helped invent. What the hell else can you do, when there's no future left to forecast and nothing to strategize for or against? A done deal. The end of history.

Adam ate some more capsules. He wasn't sure how many he'd had, but his intent was to swallow them until he couldn't swallow any more. He had the feeling he hadn't taken enough yet, but he couldn't remember how many he'd taken, so "enough" was turning into a bit of a bullshit metric. He swore he could hear thunder outside. Maybe a real storm had touched down. He swallowed a couple more. Swallowing was getting hard now. He dropped his hands in his lap. His legs were wet. Adam leaned his head down, which was a project in itself at this point. The water bottle hadn't spilled. He was amused to discover that he'd pissed himself without noticing.

"Fuck you all," he muttered. "I piss on all of you on behalf of the future."

Thunder rolled. It was a lovely sound. The only thing he was missing was some music, and thunder was close enough. Adam closed his eyes and listened to the invisible storm.

Ten days later, Adam was still furious. No bastard had told him Normal Head had emergency room facilities on the grounds. He ached from asshole to breakfast-time from the stomach pump, his throat was raw from intubation, and his arms were still livid from the shots of God-knows-what that they'd fired into him. He had sore spots all over the rest of his body, and he felt like he was still learning to walk again. Adam was determined not to apologize to Dickson for the split lip he'd given the orderly at some point over the last few days. He felt sure that Dickson had done something to deserve it, even though he couldn't prove it, and was secretly quite proud that he'd somehow summoned the strength to cause it. Most of the time he didn't have the energy to claw his way through standing air.

Dickson was with him now, patiently accompanying Adam on an endless shuffle toward Dr. Murgu's office. Every now and then Dickson would turn those hurt puppy eyes on Adam. Adam ignored them as completely as he could. Adam wanted to strangle him. Wanted to dig his fingers into that chubby little neck until he found something hard that he could break.

They reached Murgu's door. Dickson tapped on it and said to Adam, "I'll be back for you when you're done, okay? It's not too bad out on the patio today. And people have been asking after you."

"Fuck off," Adam said.

Dr. Murgu opened the door, and Dickson left, chewing his split lip.

"Adam," Dr. Murgu said, "I do wish you hadn't said that to poor Dickson."

"I blame him," Adam said. "He's been fucking haunting me since I got here. It must have been him who found me."

"Actually, it wasn't. It was him who carried you to the emergency medical facility. He collapsed, himself, a little while later. He'd been overdoing it, and hadn't slept in too long. Come in."

She put a hand to Adam's elbow, the way Dickson would, and guided him over to the chair in measured steps. Adam winced from a dozen complaining components as he sat. She took her own chair and her clipboard and looked at him with a smile that radiated, in Adam's view, a horrible pity.

Dr. Murgu paused and sighed to see him. She inhaled, then, through her nose, sharply, as she straightened her spine. Adam saw that she wasn't looking forward to this.

"So," she said. "I don't know how much you've been told. It was close. I was told that another ten minutes and you would have been dead."

"Better luck next time, I suppose."

"Actually, the attending doctor said you were quite bad at it, even for a first-timer, and should take up another hobby. She suggested . . ." Dr. Murgu peered at her notes. "I think this says 'violent masturbation.' With an additional note indicating that she's prepared to study that. Medically, I presume."

Adam almost smiled.

"You were doing so well, Adam. Given the condition that led to you being sent here, and the way you first presented to me, and then the whole thing with Mansfield. The meds and the nutrients had you functional so fast. I mean, you were far from fixed, as it were. But I really had high hopes. There was only one thing that was bothering me, that I had concerns that we might not get to quickly."

"Yeah."

"Yeah. The inciting event. I had a feeling that you might not have been able to talk about it even after you were on a steady keel in other respects. Contrary to what others may have said to you, we really don't like the idea of people having to live in Staging for the rest of their lives."

"Some of them seem to like it," Adam said. "Colegrave is positively thriving over there. I think Jasmin Bulat likes it here too. Being close to the forest."

"Colegrave will never be mentally robust enough to live in the outside world. If he wasn't producing work from Staging, his employers and sponsors would long ago have cut off the funding for him to stay here. And he permanently occupies an off-site habitation, which means one less person we can comfortably cycle into Staging. For every long-term Staging resident, the Director has to go hunting for more money to build more micro-homes and clear more land to set them down in, and connect them to water, internet, and electricity. Yes, I know those buildings can generate a lot of that, but it's not perfect, and health guidelines mean we have to connect them up. This isn't a magic village. Everything costs money."

"I suppose so," Adam said.

"Sad but true," Dr. Murgu said. "Jasmin's a different case entirely. In a lot of ways, she's healthier than Colegrave will ever be. But her depression is close to unmanageable. She's much too functional to live anywhere but Staging, but living anywhere other than Staging would, we all agree, kill her within a month. It's horrible, but we can't take the risk of releasing her. Again, we're all lucky she can produce useful work for her people outside."

Adam didn't know how to respond to that, or if he should, or if he even cared.

She watched his face.

"Adam, I'm being direct with you. Staging is sounding good to you right now. You need to know that you are months away from Staging, now. At best. There is one thing I can put in your file that might, *might* speed that process up. Because it might give me the tools I need to start helping you get better. I'm not bullshitting you or trying to trick you. It's my professional opinion that this thing needs to happen, and my professional experience telling me that the people I report to, who control the pace at which everything happens here, need to see this in your file. Do you believe me?"

"Sure."

"We need to talk about Windhoek, Adam. You came apart in Rotterdam, but the damage was done in Windhoek, in Namibia. I want you to tell me, as best you can, what happened there that hurt you."

Tears prickled Adam's eyes. "I don't want to."

"I know. But I think you have to, now. I think now is the absolute best time to do it."

"Has this room been cleaned? I mean, of insects or anything else? Did you see them do it?"

"This room has been cleaned five times since we found out, Adam. I saw the first, third, and final cleanings. You should feel good about that. Everything's fine here now."

"Okay. Okay."

"Why were you in Windhoek, Adam?"

"Okay." Adam rubbed his face with both hands, hard enough to make his skin sting. "I've been doing field research on subjects around ad hoc community generation in urban contexts. It's not new. People have been picking at it since the days of flash mobs. Occupy Wall Street was a thing, too. European protesters using BlackBerry Messenger to organize. Every now and then, some interested party will drop researchers into the field to see how it's all changing and evolving. Usually, for me, it's people who want to see how groups come together, how they can be supported, why the groups have the lives of mayflies, what kind of digital systems they use. You get the idea. One time I had to follow protesters for a company who wanted to put a mesh networking app on their phones so the protesters could crowdfund health insurance payments on the go. Insane."

Adam found a little chuckle at his calling that insane.

"Is that what you were doing in Windhoek?" Dr. Murgu asked.

Adam's little chuckle died as a rasp in his throat.

He took a deep breath.

"There's been a slow burn of unrest in Namibia for the last few years. A protester got shot dead the other summer. The elections that winter didn't do much for it. High unemployment, lots of weird sociopolitical tensions. There's a whole subsection of youth who were orphaned during their war for independence, and they weren't being looked after by the state. The U.S. State Department calls it a 'critical crime threat location,' which always kind of stuck in my head as a great piece of, you know, official language."

Adam paused. Dr. Murgu said, "Namibia's one of those places I know next to nothing about."

"I sometimes think," Adam said, "that places like Namibia are one of those dark funhouse mirrors for Americans. Americans are all about 'supporting our troops,' until those troops come home, and the best those troops can expect is some idiot mouthing 'Thank you for your service.' Because the moment they come home, they're abandoned and forgotten by the system. Unless there's a VA hospital available to kill them in. Now look at Namibia. Those kids should have the trump card. The children of fallen independence fighters. Any of us would say that they should be sitting on fucking thrones. But it's America's abandonment of its troops multiplied by a hundred. Makes me wonder how the children of the Confederate and Union Armies got along after the Civil War. Probably not much better, I suppose."

"So it was dangerous in Windhoek?"

"Petty street crime, mostly. Even the street protests are largely unarmed beyond sticks and stones and whatever they can pick up along the way."

"And you were there to watch the protests?"

"Internet access in Namibia mostly comes through other countries, and there are still a lot of GSM phones. The way people use phones, texts, messaging, and email . . . Well, anyway, there were interested companies. You get a lot of user experience designers interested in this stuff, which always seems odd to other people. I was there to hang around the city for a few days, talk to people, watch how communication happened on the street."

"So you were in the middle of a protest."

"The last night I was there. A big one kicked off in central Windhoek. It was, um . . ."

"Don't disappear into visualizing it, Adam. Keep talking to me. Tell me what it was like. Hot? Cold?"

"Foggy. Very foggy night. The fog blows in off the desert, I think. I'm told it's been getting worse over the last few years. Big fogs at the wrong time of year. Usual story. City gets smacked by fog at an unseasonable time of year, and some idiot politician says, 'Ho ho, it's cold in summer, so much for this global warming people talk about, eh?' But, yeah. Cold and foggy. Which never stopped any decent protester. So people were out on the streets in force."

"What was their mood? Angry? Aggressive?"

"Angry, sure. You don't organize a protest unless you're pissed off at some level. Also nervous. There'd been a lot of talk about the Windhoek City Police falling back in favor of the Special Field Force, and they don't have a great history when it comes to peacekeeping, understanding city folk, or being smart enough to climb out of a paper bag without using guns. They wear masks. You'd be nervous."

"I would be. Were you?"

"I was . . . edgy? I'd had a weird few months. Cryptic emails and subtweets about some of my old work. One of the other guys at the nonprofit I work for lost his shit about eight weeks before I went to Windhoek."

Dr. Murgu looked at the top sheet of Adam's file again, frowning. "Is he here?"

"No. He disappeared. Everyone thought he'd killed himself or was wandering the streets. Turned out he pulled a geographic. Attended some tiny conference in Mount Vernon, left all his stuff in the motel room, rented a car, and drove an hour up I-5 to the Canadian border crossing at Sumas. It's another hour from there to Vancouver, and by evening he was on a plane to Holland, where waiting for him was a schizophrenic teenage girl who thought he was Nostradamus. There was no chance of getting him here, and by that point nobody was really that into the idea anymore. I understand he's selling his blood for spending money at this point, but . . ."

"But," Dr. Murgu said, with a gentle smile, "that's not why we're here today."

"I guess not," Adam said. "I was edgy. Something just felt wrong, and I couldn't put a finger on it. General low-level anxiety, I suppose, would be a fair way to describe it."

"You were in the middle of the protest," she prompted.

"No, actually. I was on the edge of it, when it happened. The core of it was moving fast, and I'd come into the group from the wrong side. So, between the fog, and stragglers, and not knowing the streets that well, I was falling behind a little bit. I'm usually better with street layout. I usually plan better, I mean. I learn the layout off maps. But I wasn't feeling that great, and there wasn't signal to run a map app on my phone, and in any case taking an expensive smartphone out in that kind of place and situation is pretty stupid. I wasn't quite bumping around, lost in the fog, but, you know . . . a bit. And . . . that's when it happened."

Adam paused for a minute, and then said, "That's when I met the man who wasn't there."

Dr. Murgu just waited.

"Do you know that poem?" Adam asked. "'Antigonish.' I just remembered that it's supposed to be about a haunted house in Canada. 'Yesterday, upon the stair, / I met a man who wasn't there.'"

"'He wasn't there again today,'" Dr. Murgu said, "'I wish, I wish he'd go away.'"

Adam closed his eyes. He could see it again.

"Talk to me, Adam," she said. "Tell me what you're remembering."

"There was this guy. He was hanging back from the edge of it all, same as me. But I kept seeing him. I realized he wasn't trying to catch up. He was deliberately keeping pace but keeping his distance. It was foggy. The lights were all smeary—the streetlights, car headlamps, flares people kept setting off. It was hard to see. And this guy, he was heavyset. Couldn't see his hands. He was always facing the crowd. And I remember thinking, this guy's trouble. Something about him is just off. I got this whole secret-police vibe off him."

"Did you confront him?"

"That seemed like a really, really bad idea. If I was right, then he was armed, and in direct communication with a team, because those people don't wander into the field on their own. But it didn't matter. I did something even more stupid than that."

She raised an eyebrow.

"The pack broke. I still don't know what happened. It sounded like firecrackers going off, but it could have been small-caliber gunfire or any of half a dozen other things. And my position was that the only way out of the surge of people coming toward me was an alley on the other side of the street that that guy had planted himself in front of. I didn't want to turn around and run the other way because I knew there was a police cordon a block or two back. I had no idea if the entire crowd was running. I went for the best option, which was ducking out of its way. So I ran across the street. Grabbed the guy's arms to guide myself around him without knocking him flat as I twisted into the mouth of the alley."

Adam flexed and splayed his fingers in front of him, as if they could still feel it. The memory of fog.

"His arms came apart in my hands. The surge had stopped—whatever it was, it turned out the crowd just wanted to get distance from it and then gawp. So nobody there was looking at us. I lost my balance a bit, because I didn't have anything to hold on to as I twisted around the guy. I remember my arms flailing. I remember my arm passing almost all the way through him. My wrist bounced off something plastic, and it hurt. I pulled my arm out. And my arm was inside him. There was nothing of him. Just something moving around inside the space of him. And . . . he was fog."

"Fog."

"Yeah. My flailing around dispersed him, sort of. And even in that bad light, I could see what he was. What he really was. You have to understand, this is real. This isn't me describing a hallucination. I had the mark on my wrist. My clothes smelled of the spray afterward, and I hadn't been near any other chemicals. I recognized some of what I was looking at. It was as real as this room and this chair."

"Tell me," Dr. Murgu said, "what it was."

"It sounds ridiculous. It was a ridiculous thing to get upset about," Adam said, his voice cracking.

"Tell me."

"It was micro-drones. Tiny quadcopters. And they

were spraying fog. Well, not fog; it was clouds of atomized chemicals that were draping around them. They were traveling in formation, a vertical stack of them, and spraying a chemical shroud and projecting an image on the spray from the inside. In that weather? In that lighting? It passed for a big guy in a long heavy coat who you didn't want to go near. The drones had some kind of coating on them that made them hard to look at. I realized later that it would have been a metamaterial cladding. You've seen the news stories about making things nearly invisible. It's done with metamaterials that change the way light works. It was just a cloud of drones tracking a crowd of protesters at street level."

"A man who wasn't there," she said.

"And, oh my God, I want him to go away," he said.

Dr. Murgu thought for a moment, jotting down a few sentences on her clipboard. She then said, "When you saw Mr. Mansfield—"

"It wasn't a person."

"We don't have a better label for him. It. Whatever. But okay. When you saw it, did you guess what you were looking at? Right at the start?"

"No. It bothered me. But I didn't know what it was, not until we smashed an insect."

"Did you suspect?"

"I don't think I wanted to. When you wish a man who isn't there would go away, the last idea you want to entertain is that there are more like him. That's what I couldn't get out of my head in Windhoek and Rotterdam. Because if you're going to make flights of microdrones with fog camouflage so they can blend into urban street-level backgrounds at mid-distance, is Windhoek in Namibia the only place you're ever going to fly them? There are foggy, rainy, cloudy, smoky cities all over the world. There are cities with narrower streets, more bends and curves, riddled with more alleyways and ratholes. If you're working with projections and sprays and metamaterials, then it doesn't even make sense to use human-shaped camouflage in most instances. If the man who wasn't there was a test article, then I would bet you real money that the only test involved was the shape. No. Those things are going to be everywhere. Half-visible, half-autonomous, and networked."

"Half-autonomous?"

"The thing reassembled itself in front of me. A swarm of flying robots went back into formation on its own. That's algorithmic. How deep does that go? The swarm could respond to my action of waving my arm around to disperse them by returning to formation. How does it react when a crowd surges toward it? I don't know. I might have found out, if the crowd had kept moving. My point is, there are things it can do on its own without being instructed from afar, because the action was too quick to have required a human operator. And, in fact, you don't put something like that into the field if it *needs* a human operator."

"Stop and take a breath, Adam."

Adam realized his chest was heaving. He rushed on. He needed it out of him. "I came up with a way to strike targets using tiny drones with explosive charges inside. Either what I bumped into was a cloud of spotters for Stoop Model drones above the scene. Or I bumped into a cloud of actual kill vehicles. Think about that. You're in a protest, or a riot, a mass of people. And then one of the people vanishes, and the next second twelve people are dead."

Adam took his breath, looking at Dr. Murgu resentfully from under his brow. He said, "The thing about the future is that it keeps happening without you."

"You thought of something that had evolved under other hands after you left that particular field. Here, you encountered something that sounds like it may have been a further evolution of this idea of drone devices operating under human camouflage. Yes?"

"Yes. I'd never even thought of what they did here. Whoever they are. And that's the thing, isn't it? We always say 'they.' I had a stepfather for a few years who used 'they' all the time because it was a magical buttress to any old shit he came up with. The first time he hit me. One summer. He poured my mother a glass of lemonade with this bullshit flourish, and said, 'They reckon lemonade cools you down more than anything.' And I asked who 'they' were. Was it the same 'they' who let black people live anywhere they liked? Because he'd had a fair amount to say about that 'they.' Same 'they' who gave away jobs to kids with tattoos and pins in their noses? Or the same 'they' who got in the way of everyone having a big war to sort everything out? Because 'they' were probably a bunch of morons. He followed me out of the room, put his left hand over my mouth, and punched me in the stomach with his right. There, see? Real therapy stuff. Talking about my childhood."

"Your point being we never really know who's doing what. The nature of government?"

"Government is barely the tip of the iceberg now. Non-state actors, asymmetrical warfighters, skunkworks, security multinationals, who the hell knows. We lost the battle for our streets a long time ago. We gave them up. Worse: we gave up the ideas and data freely to the people who used them to take our streets from us. Do you understand exactly what that thing in Mansfield's room tells us? It tells us that we quite literally have no idea what is loose in the world and looking at and listening to us, and who it is looking and listening for. Bugs as bugs. It's fucking comedy. There's a whole boardroom full of people who were shitting themselves laughing at that. A hundred and eighty pounds of semiautonomous mobile listening devices in human form. No wonder you

never got a physical examination or a one-on-one interview out of him. But note, very carefully, how it was
otherwise convincing enough to your staff and the
people who live here. The future arrived here a couple of
weeks ago and nobody noticed. Because that's how the
future always arrives. You don't realize it's here until you
bump into it."

"You helped solve it, Adam. You achieved something. Do you understand? Staging tracked the remaining devices that tried to call home and upload their
recordings. Everyone else grabbed the fake investigators
when they arrived to get an on-site upload and collect
the things up. They were from a private intelligence anal-
ysis company that doesn't have access to Normal Head
production. There's a whole investigation now. Other
countries are implicated. And, while it was concluding,
you tried quite hard to kill yourself. Can you tell me
something about what you were thinking as you did
that?"

"Oh." Adam tried to laugh derisively, but the sound
strangled in his throat. "That was the easy part. That was
the easy decision. It was the confirmation of my night-
mare. We're now in a place, you see, where we will never
again have a private conversation. We're never really
going to be alone again. We will never again be in a state
where we believe that we're not being watched. Some

futurists talk about a thing called the Singularity, where accelerating progress in technology becomes a runaway effect. Like an ascending graph that suddenly becomes a vertical straight line. Think of a Surveillance Singularity. A condition you cannot go back from, because it's become a runaway effect, like critical mass in a reactor."

"Maybe it was just being tested here, Adam. A small, remote place to see if it worked. Just like a fairly peaceful protest in Namibia would be a good place to test a prototype technology."

"Maybe. But maybe it wasn't. Maybe these are just the tools 'they' use now. Maybe this is just the world we live in, and nobody's noticed yet. But I have. I worked for it. I tried to kill myself because I don't want to live in a world like that. I don't want to spend my life wondering who's copying down everything I say and who it will be used to hurt. I don't want that. I don't want to be in that world."

"Adam. You don't live in the world anymore. You live in Normal. The only people watching are us now. This is a safe place."

"You hesitated, there," Adam said. "You were going to say something else."

"I was going to say," Dr. Murgu said, "that this is the last safe place."

Adam Dearden racked his brains for something to

say that would get him out of this room and away so that he could conceive a proper process to do it again and do it right. He was a clever man. He was paid to think about the future all day, every day. He should, he figured, be able to work out a plan to escape it.

ACKNOWLEDGMENTS

This little book is for, and because of, my many friends and acquaintances in the business of the future. Their work and lives gave me the idea, and I owe them all a drink, but none of them should carry the blame.